570

3 1

D0629978

Pat's Harmony

Pat's

Cleveland and New York

Harmony

by PAGE COOPER

Introduction by CLOUD L. CRAY

Illustrated by OLIVER GRIMLEY

THE WORLD PUBLISHING COMPANY

Library of Congress Catalog Card Number: 52–8424

FIRST EDITION

HC 8 52

Copyright 1952 by The World Publishing Company

to Pat

Introduction

Readers of this story about a girl and the horse she loved may like to know that it is true. For several years Harmony, the big chestnut hunter and jumper, was well known to horsemen throughout America, and the girl who trained and rode him to many a victory in the horse shows was my daughter Patricia Lee.

With the privilege of fiction we have changed somewhat the setting of Pat's life, for she did not grow up on a ranch like the Pat of the story, but she did live with horses from the time she could walk out to the paddock. As for Harmony, the story follows his adventures closely. The colt did survive a bitter winter lost in a canyon, and was nursed back to health by a neighbor's wife who rescued him from being shot and gave him the care which Pat does in this book. The photograph on the jacket shows what a sorry wreck he was when they found him in the spring: mud-caked, starved, rickety, not worth the powder to shoot him. This is the horse that Pat developed into one of the outstanding jumpers and working hunters in the Midwest. Harmony came to her when she was fourteen. She fed him, groomed him and trained him, and he responded with all the devotion of which his great heart was capable. Although he was an easy, good-tem-

pered horse that anyone could ride, he never jumped for anyone else the way he did for Pat.

One of the largest dealers in training and selling jumpers and
hunters made the remark that he had never seen a horse take
care of its rider in horse shows as Harmony took care of Pat.
I recall distinctly the show in Grand Rapids, Michigan, in the
spring of 1949 when Pat was sixteen. Pat was showing Harmony
and Lady Luck, and one other young mare called Taffy. Because of inexperience, Taffy had a bad fall at a jump and Pat
was knocked unconscious with a slight concussion. Two events
later was the hunter stake in which Harmony was entered.
When we told Pat she was in no condition to ride she became
hysterical and the doctor advised that it might be best to let her
ride. Harmony seemed to sense that something was wrong; he
took the jumps with unusual care. Although he won against
stiff competition, Pat to this day does not recall riding in that
event.

Pat rode Harmony in horse shows from Kansas City's classic
"American Royal" to Madison Square Garden, and Harmony
was a regular attendant at shows in Detroit, Chicago, Columbus,
Fort Wayne, and almost all of the shows in Michigan. When
requested Pat often gave exhibitions of bareback riding like the
ones described in the story. Pat's trophy room is full of trophies
won by Harmony and Lady Luck, who was his team-mate in
most of the shows attended. The ribbons won by these two horses
total several hundred.

In these adventures of Harmony and Pat we have tried to
capture the relationship between our Pat and her Harmony: a
relationship in which a girl and a horse love and trust and give
their best to each other.

CLOUD L. CRAY

Contents

[ix]

Illustrations

Pat's Harmony

Chapter 1

Harmony Comes Home

The doe jumped out of the thicket of buffalo berries along the draw and bounced over the hill, her tail sticking up like a white plume between her silver flanks. Watching her, the girl threw back her head and laughed. Pat Cole, just turned thirteen, was as restive with the stir of spring as the yearlings kicking up their heels around the water hole. All about her stretched the prairie, ripples of little hills, greenish-gold and fawn except where clumps of bushes in the draws lay across them like the shadows of giant fingers. They went on and on forever; not a house, not a barn in sight, not a human anywhere under the mild, cloudless sky.

This was the way the prairie looked when the Indians roamed it. Pat liked to think of herself as a pioneer, the first white woman to see the land all new and sweet-smelling like a fresh loaf from God's oven. And so it was, almost, for no plow had disturbed the buffalo grass turning green under the May sun. Not even a fence crossed the eye. Until she reached the second rise ahead and came in sight of Ty Chisholm's barns, she might have been Granny Thurston, years ago, walking ahead of her oxcart, maybe picking a handful of gumbo lilies and sticking one in her hair.

Once when Pat and her father and mother were on a picnic in the buttes—they had come upon a patch of the lilies on a high plain that topped the hills, and Margaret, her mother, had stuck one in her dark coronet of braids. Glancing at her there on the edge of the cliffs, with the world spread at her feet, Pat had thought, "She is like Eve in the Bible story looking out over the garden of Eden and this is the way the world looked when it began." So when she pictured Granny walking these prairies as a bride with never another woman nearer than Fort Pierre, she saw her with a gumbo lily in her hair.

The girl looked for dry clay flats as she walked along the cow-path and found a drift of the lilies, waxy white in their dark-green sheaths. She picked one and stuck it into her braid near the end where it curled up in a pigtail. Make-believe was a game with endless possibilities. She imagined herself choosing a hill beyond the creek where the willows were thick, and saying to Grandpa, "Here is where I want my house." And she would play making jackets and mittens for Grandpa out of antelope skins, or cooking venison steaks over a fire of dried buffalo dung. Sometimes she imagined herself cutting a wild pony out of a herd and breaking it for her own. It was always a chestnut pony with two white stockings on his hind legs, a spot of white on one front pastern and a white star and strip on his face. A wild pony wouldn't have been likely to have such markings, but in make-believe you can arrange everything the way you want it. The play pony always looked like Harmony, the thoroughbred colt that had almost been hers.

Whatever game she played, her thoughts came back to the chestnut colt and to her father, Sketch, and the fun they had had together. For a little while, out in the middle of the prairie with no one in sight but the horses and the meadow larks that she flushed along the path, the girl was happy. The lead was lifted from her heart, but as she topped a rise and came in sight of Ty Chisholm's barns and corrals, it settled again, the dull loneliness for her father that she couldn't lose anywhere.

It was seven months now since Sketch Cole had died, killed in an Eastern rodeo. They had sent him home in a coffin. The girl didn't remember much about the coffin and the funeral, there was too much confusion, too many people going in and out of the house. After it was over Pat and her mother had opened the box in which someone had sent her father's tackle, his bridles and silver-mounted saddle. Under them, packed in the wrappings in which it had come from the harness shop, they found a small English saddle—the gift he had promised his daughter to replace the tiny nine-pound saddle that Doc had given her on her eighth birthday. She had outgrown the old one and the stuffing was coming out.

If he won good money at the rodeos, Sketch had promised to bring Pat a riding habit and all the trimmings. He didn't want his daughter to grow up to be a cowgirl riding in jeans, with a kerchief around her neck. She should have a thoroughbred, a jumper, and she should ride in the horse shows like the girls he had seen in the East.

Last summer he had schooled her on one of his gentlest horses, teaching her to ride the forward seat, showing her how to take the horse over a barrel or a low rail set on a couple of boxes. And all summer long they had looked for the right horse for her, making a game of it. Ty Chisholm, who was the only breeder of thoroughbreds in this part of South Dakota, would come along with them. Sketch and Ty used to take the carryall or Sketch's Ford and go barging across the far pastures, where there were no roads except old cattle trails, pretending to look for gaps in the fences but mostly talking horses and watching the foals and yearlings grazing by their dams. Once in a while Sketch would say, "Pat, how would you like that one?" pointing out a strawberry roan colt or a gray. But he could never change her mind. The one she wanted was a chestnut yearling with two white feet. She had fallen in love with him the first time she saw him in the pasture. Sometimes the colt would let her get so close that she could give him a carrot or a handful of grass.

"But I've seen horses with better conformation," Sketch would urge. "Don't you want a perfect horse?"

"Stop trying to kid the child," Ty would say. "That's a good colt and you can't fool her. He's a full brother to Music, and the fellow who bought her has been grabbing off the ribbons all year at Fort Wayne and Memphis and Kansas City. Guess this one should have a musical name. What shall we call him, Pat? Harmony?"

"Yes, yes," Pat agreed eagerly. "That's a beautiful name. Harmony! I could call him Harm for short."

Sketch, seeing the longing in the child's eyes, would curl her pigtails around his finger. "You shall have him, honey. I promise. A yearling's too skittish for you to handle but next spring I'll break him for you. And you keep an eye on this big four-flusher and see that he doesn't double cross you."

"Don't you worry, kid," Ty would say, patting her on the shoulder. "He'll be waiting for you next spring, winter-fed and as plump as a possum."

If only Pat could stop thinking about last fall. But there it was, always like a great lump on her chest. She was waiting at Ty Chisholm's the day they drove the horses in from the Slim Buttes. It was November, the wind tore out of the north, spitting snow that swept low across the hills, racing down the slopes in crested spume. She had been in Ma Chisholm's kitchen eating a doughnut and watching out the window for the horses to come in, hoping she'd catch a glimpse of Harmony; she hadn't been able to see a thing until Jake, Ty's son, blew through the kitchen door. Ma poured him a cup of coffee.

"Get 'em all in?" Pat asked.

"All but Roanne and Harmony."

Pat could still feel how she had trembled inside.

"What happened to Harmony?"

Jake had stood by the kitchen stove warming his hands on his coffee cup.

"Gee, I hate to tell you, kid. A wolf must have got Roanne, a wolf or a lynx cat. Must have hamstrung her and driven her from the herd. We found her bones at the end of a draw, picked clean by the coyotes. Hasn't been a wolf in this country for a dozen years, but one might have wandered across the buttes from Wyoming. He must have got Harmony, too, although we didn't find a trace of him. Maybe he got farther away. We looked the best we could but didn't have any luck. The chestnut's dead now for sure, so you forget about him, honey. First warm day I'll show you the cutest little black colt you ever laid your eyes on."

Pat had burst into tears. She had tried not to, but she couldn't help it. Ma Chisholm had pressed the girl against her fat, comforting side and put another cookie in her hand, but it didn't taste good splattered with salt tears.

"You're going to have another colt, dear, one a lot better than Harmony. Don't you think about him any more."

But Pat couldn't help it. Every night when she closed her eyes she saw the frightened colt running up a draw and the wolf leaping from a ledge above. Sometimes it was so real that she woke up gasping from holding her breath.

That was after Sketch had gone away. Then when his saddle had come home, his beautiful parade saddle with the silver trimmings, the bottom had fallen out of her world. At first she couldn't believe that she would never see Sketch again, never hear the heels of his boots tapping across the kitchen in the morning when he called to her: "Get up, lazybones, and drink your milk. We've got to go out and look after the horses," never watch his slim, swaggering figure leaning against the gate of the corral or see the light that danced behind his eyes when he smiled. At first she watched for him, making herself believe she'd see him come riding up the road from Strool. But when she looked at her mother she knew that they would never have those happy times again. Margaret moved about the house as though she were a wooden doll. She said "yes" and "no" when Pat spoke to her, but she was all locked up in herself as though she were shut in a room without any windows. She sold Sketch's horses, sent them to the market at Belle Fourche, every one of them, and sold the silver saddle to a rodeo rider from Wyoming. With the money she fenced in more pasture and bought more sheep. They were all a woman could tend to on a ranch, she said. Sketch had hated the sheep and laughed at their silly faces, but Margaret had made a little money from them. Now she had cleaned out the barn and given away Sketch's tackle, all but a hunting bridle which Pat had kept for her English saddle. It was as though Margaret had tried to get rid of everything that had belonged to Sketch.

Pat couldn't understand her mother. In her desperate loneliless she had yearned toward Margaret, but she could never break down the wall. Sometimes Margaret caught the child in a hard embrace and burst into fits of weeping but these shut Pat out further than the wooden silences.

Then school had started. All winter long she had ridden through the snow to the snug little one-room school down the road, and during the day her playmates had helped her to forget about Sketch. But now she was at home all day with Margaret, and every gate, every fence post, every willow along the creek emphasized her loneliness.

The only one who understood was Ma Chisholm. That was one reason Pat never missed mail day. Twice a week the postman brought mail to the Chisholm ranch for the neighborhood. There was seldom anything for the Coles but an advertisement or a postcard from her mother's sister in Colorado. Now that it

was spring, Pat liked to walk across the prairie through patches
of white flowering peppergrass, and feel the timid May sun on
her face.

As Pat climbed the last rise behind the Chisholm house she
saw a truck coming across the prairie. She sat down beside the
path and waited for it. The clear air was deceptive; although it
looked as though you could almost touch the truck, she knew
that it was about three miles away. It was Jake's truck and she
loved to ride up front with him. She wanted to ask what horses
were in the corral and if she could ride one of them.

When the truck came within shouting distance, Pat jumped
up and called, "Hi."

"Hi, yourself," Jake answered. "Where did you pop up from
just like a jack rabbit?" He clanked to a stop for her to jump
in. "What you guess I've got in back?"

She looked through the glass in the back of the cab. Lying in
a heap on the floor was the saddest-looking colt she'd ever seen.
His hip bones stuck out like little peaks and he was covered
from his eyes to his tail with caked mud. You couldn't tell his
color.

"Poor thing. What happened to him?" she asked Jake.

"Don't you recognize him? That's Harmony. Guess the wolf
didn't get him after all, but how he lived through the winter is
anybody's guess. I found him half-dead like this when we
turned the horses out into the far pasture this morning and
took out the truck to bring him in although there really isn't
any use. He's most dead anyhow."

"No, no," Pat cried. "Let me down. I want to get in back."
Jake stopped and boosted Pat into the body of the truck. She sat
on the floor and lifted the colt's head into her lap, smearing her
jeans with mud. With the kerchief from her head she tried to
wipe out his watering eyes that were caked and half closed.
They were sunk so deep that they looked as if they were about
to fall inside his head. They were open but you couldn't tell

They looked at the pitiful skeleton.

whether they were looking at anything. Gently she scrubbed at his face, trying to clean the white star.

When they drew into the corral, Ty Chisholm came out with Doc Carr, the vet who usually managed to drop in about the time Ma took hot biscuits from the oven. They let down the tailboard and looked curiously at the pitiful skeleton.

"Jump down, honey. Look what you've got on your jeans." Ty helped Pat out and leaned his square, wind-reddened face over the colt. He prodded it with a mighty finger but it was too weak to quiver.

"He can hardly stand up," Jake said, unwinding his long frame from the cab. "Didn't have enough strength to keep on his legs." They lifted out the colt who looked at them with glassy eyes and stood wobbling on legs that promised to buckle at any minute.

"What'd we better do with him, Doc? Shoot him? He hasn't got a chance."

"Might as well. Even if he lives he's been so undernourished that he'll never develop good bone."

Patty threw her arms around the colt's head.

"No, no, you can't shoot him. This is my horse. Sketch promised him to me."

"Well, if that isn't Sketch's girl for you. Now don't get excited, honey." Old Doc gave her pigtails a twist. "If you want him that badly I expect Ty will give him to you."

"Sure," the big man said. "She's welcome to him—he isn't worth shooting—but you know Margaret isn't going to want him on the place. She won't have any horse, let alone a wreck like him. Now that she blames every horse she sees for what happened to Sketch she isn't going to give this ghost stable room."

The vet nodded.

"It isn't fair. This kid's been mad about horses since she was knee-high to a grasshopper and suddenly everything's wiped out: Sketch, the horses, all the fun they used to have. It's pretty tough on such a young kid. Give the colt to her, Ty. Maybe I can help pull him through."

Ty nodded slowly, then he grinned.

"Will you square me with Margaret?"

Doc took off his old cavalry hat and scratched his head. Then he began to whistle a march.

"Forward, the light brigade," he grunted.

Pat, who had been looking from one to the other, holding her breath, caught Doc's arm and squeezed it tight.

"I love you," she burst out, "I love you. I'll soap your saddle every week and I'll . . . I'll . . ."

Doc laughed.

"Don't tax yourself to think of anything else. We haven't got around your mother yet. I'd better give the colt a shot to keep him on his feet."

Doc took a worn leather case out of his pocket and extracted a hypodermic needle.

"Here, Patty, run into the kitchen and stick this into some boiling water. And, Jake, maybe you'll make a hot bran mash for him. We've got to get a little strength in him somehow."

Pat dashed into the kitchen and came back carrying the needle in a pan of boiling water. Doc fished it out, filled the holder with liquid from a tiny bottle that he carried in another case and stuck it into the colt behind his shoulder. The poor creature gave a spasmodic jerk and twitched his ears. In a few seconds he seemed to be steadier on his feet.

"Come on into the kitchen," Ty said, "while Jake makes the mash. I smell Ma's coffee."

Doc took Pat's hand and drew her with them. The two men sat at the kitchen table: Ty, a crag of a man, slow, quiet, as majestic as one of his Hereford bulls; Doc, small, compact, dapper, erect as a ramrod. Ma had the oven door open and was just taking out a pan of biscuits that she whisked onto a large plate on the table.

"Well, if here isn't the fugitive from the Rough Riders looking for a handout. They must have starved you in the army, son."

Doc tossed his old cavalry hat on the floor. The feud between Ma and him was one of their constant pleasures.

"Well now, let's see." Doc split a biscuit and laced it with a hunk of butter. "Pity we didn't have these at San Juan Hill. We'd have killed a lot more Spaniards."

Pat didn't listen to their bandying, she wiggled impatiently on the edge of her chair. Why did they keep talking on and on, never saying anything? She looked at the calendar above the table, showing a blonde girl with a bunch of roses in her hand, and the coyote skin behind Ma's sewing machine, its green felt mounting making bright scallops on the whitewashed wall. She looked at the cupboard where Ma kept her best cups that nobody ever drank out of, except at parties, and then back at the table where Ty and Doc were stirring sugar into their coffee.

Doc was grinning at Ma and twisting his cavalry moustache. Pat tried to keep her eyes from the door but finally she could stand it no longer.

"I'll be in the corral," she whispered to Doc. He squeezed her hand without looking up. She ran across the yard, scattering the chickens and almost stepping on Ma's lazy old cat. Filling a bucket with warm water from the tank that had been heating in the sun, she carried it to the colt, then ran to the stable for a cloth. First she sponged the colt's eyes, his poor sunken oozing eyes, then she began on his face. He stirred a little and flicked an ear. Presently the white star and strip began to show beneath the mud. The afternoon sang with a hundred voices, the lazy buzzing of flies, the panting of an old horse trying to lap up some spilled oats with his wide black lips, the clucking of Ma's turkeys strutting behind the corral, the twittering of swallows in the barn; but loudest of all, Pat's heart was singing. She could hear it pounding against her ribs as though it would burst from happiness. And the song it sang was "Harmony, honey, you belong to me."

Chapter 2

"If She Really Loves Me"

Presently Doc came out of the kitchen wiping his cavalry moustache. Jake had brought a pan of warm mash and he and Pat had helped the colt eat it, first putting a little on his tongue, then watching him nibble it, his loose black lips working awkwardly as though his jaws were old hinges caked with rust.

Jake sat the gangplank over the edge of Doc's pickup, a long-bodied car with wooden racks on the sides.

"Up he goes." With Doc on one side and Jake on the other, the colt was half pushed, half lifted into the pickup where he stood uncertainly, still working his lips. Doc brushed off his hands with his handkerchief. He bargained with Jake for two bags of oats and a couple of bran, which Jake brought from the barn and stacked against the tailboard. Doc slid under the wheel, put his foot on the starter and held open the door for Pat.

From the kitchen door Ty saluted with his giant hand, calling, "I wouldn't risk more than a plugged nickel on your chances with Margaret."

The pickup wheeled out of the yard into a faint road that snaked across the prairie. When it came to a fence gate, three strands of wire hitched to a couple of poles, Pat jumped down and loosened one pole from the wire loops that held it, then set

it back again when Doc had driven through. She never took her
eyes from the colt, afraid each jolt would throw him off his feet.

"Stop worrying, Patty. He's going to be all right."

"But even if he is, she won't let me have him. When I wanted
to keep one of Sketch's colts, she said no, I'd just have to understand it was horses that killed Sketch. If he hadn't been so horse
crazy he would still be here safe on the ranch. I was all she had
left and she couldn't risk having me go horse crazy too. Then
she hugged me so tight she scared me and said she never wanted
to talk about it again."

Pat looked up at Doc with troubled eyes.

"But I *don't* understand. It isn't crazy to want a horse. Sketch
intended me to have one. He always did. Sometimes I think she
doesn't even love me. She won't talk to me. She doesn't know
I'm there. I get frightened. But honestly I haven't done anything to make her angry with me. Doc, why doesn't she love
me any more?"

Doc opened his mouth to reply, then thought better of it, took
a cigar out of his vest pocket and chewed thoughtfully on the
tip.

"Patty, you're almost grown up now," he began finally, "and
I'm going to talk to you as if you were. Margaret and Sketch
loved each other as much as two people can, but they were
very different. Maybe that's the reason they cared so much.
They didn't see life the same way. Margaret had the ranch.
You know it belonged to your grandfather. He worked terribly
hard for it, through the bitter winters and droughts, fighting
off wolves and coyotes and blackleg and distemper. Every time
he saved a little he put it into the ranch, built the new log house
so your grandmother wouldn't have to live in a soddy, and put
up the barn and corrals. Your mother remembers those hard
times. She wanted to sit down on the ranch and live a nice
safe life with Sketch at home looking after the cattle and mend-
ing fences and perhaps every year doing a little more for the

ranch—putting in bottled gas, all the things Ma Chisholm and the neighbors have. She wanted to hold tight to what she had and make everything snug for you and Sketch. It was a woman's way to look at things, Pat. Most of them want to hold on to what they have."

The girl's eyes followed a sage hen rising heavily from a clump of grass but she did not see the bird, she was remembering Sketch practicing in the corral, clinging to the horns of an outraged steer. Everything he did was thrilling. When he got his gear together in the fall he made Pat's eyes glow with tales of the fabulous places he was going to see; and when he came home with a carful of presents, it was better than Christmas. Even going on a picnic with him was something special for he made you notice the things around you, the birds and the jack rabbits and antelope, and he told you stories about them so the prairie or the buttes, wherever you happened to be, was all at once a different and marvelous place.

"I know he didn't like to stay at home very well. Maybe he didn't want to be safe."

"That's it." Doc took another chew on the end of his cigar and spoke slowly, feeling for the right words. "He just had to have action and excitement. I don't think it ever occurred to him that your mother would rather have a bathtub than the fancy car he brought home last year. He lived every minute. He wanted you to have a good time now and he didn't think much about what was going to happen ten or twenty years from now. And your mother, she said he was horse crazy. He was, but even if horses had never been born he wouldn't have settled down at home like a tame cat. Your mother couldn't see that. She blamed it all on horses. It was a horse that killed him and she's going to be very sure that you're not going to be horse crazy too. You're all she has, Pat."

"But if she really loves me, wouldn't you think she would let me have what I want most in the world?"

Doc shook his head.

"Love's a funny thing. I'm old enough to be your grand-daddy and I don't understand it yet, so don't you try. You should have your colt and I think I can fix it. But no matter how Margaret acts, don't doubt for one minute that she loves you."

Pat sighed.

"I think I'll die if she doesn't let me have Harmony."

They reached the gate to the Coles' front pasture. As Pat shut it, she glanced anxiously toward the house but no one was in sight. The old log building lay low and snug on top of a ridge, its walls of giant light cottonwood blending with the tones of the buffalo grass. Behind it, the faded red barn and the faded red corrals, the Slim Buttes rose, ridges of hills perpendicular, stripped of earth except on top where they were spotted with stunted pines and wind carved like the battlements of ancient castles. It was a long way yet across the field. With mounting dread Pat watched the pickup shortening the undulating meadow. She moved closer to Doc; he patted her arm.

"I'm scared too, honey, but we mustn't show it."

The car halted at the small corral that opened from the barn.

"We'll put Harmony in the corral; you keep out of the way while I go in and talk with Margaret. Finish cleaning him up. Maybe we can see what he looks like when you get off the mud." He smoothed his moustache, squared his shoulders and went around to the kitchen door. When Margaret opened it he stepped in quickly, pulling the screen behind him and walked toward the table steering her away from the door.

"Well, Margaret, lovely as ever. I get awfully sick of these girls with docked hair and like to come around and look at your coronet."

Margaret put her hand to the plaits of dusky hair that were twisted around her head. They gave her face a tapering heart-shaped look, like the queen on a deck of cards. She was slim

and pliant as a willow switch but too thin, Doc thought. He
didn't like the hollows under her eyes. She made a place for
him at the table and put the coffeepot on the front of the stove.

"You're just in time. I've made a batch of cookies for Pat.
She isn't having much fun this summer."

Doc eyed the coffeepot with misgivings, he was full to the
throatlatch with Ma Chisholm's brew, but coffee always helped
to limber up a situation.

"Ma Chisholm just fed me a batch of her biscuits but I can't
turn down your cookies. What do you suppose Jake found in
the buttes this morning? The chestnut colt that Sketch had
promised Pat. The wolf didn't get him after all and somehow he
managed to live through the winter although he almost starved.
Ty gave him to Pat and you never saw such a happy child in
your life."

Margaret stiffened with the coffeepot in her hand.

"You mean there's a colt out there now?"

Doc nodded.

"We brought him in the pickup."

"Well, you can take him right back. We haven't any horses
on this ranch. I'm just beginning to make out on sheep and I
don't want a horse, especially a thoroughbred who will eat his
head off all winter."

"But, Margaret, Pat was promised the horse. Don't you know
how much it means to her?"

"I can't afford it, I tell you. I'm the only one left to run things
now and I've got to save every cent for her to go to school. I
just can't risk a cent until I get on my feet." She caught the
look of skepticism in his eyes. "I'm not just being difficult. I
really can't afford it, Doc."

"You don't need to worry about the expense. I'll keep the
horse in oats and bran, and the hay he eats you'll never miss.
I'd like to do that much for Pat."

Margaret whirled on him. "Handsomest woman in the county," he thought, "with anger putting a little red in her cheeks."

"Can't you see, Doc? Do I have to spell it out for you? I just don't want horses. Every time I see one I think what they did to Sketch. And I don't want Pat to be like him. I couldn't stand it, I tell you. I don't want Pat to have a horse." She ended defiant, her eyes blazing, then as she saw the compassion in Doc's face she began to crumple. Flinging herself down by the table she buried her face in her hands.

Doc wanted to get up and run; he never knew what to do about tears, at least not unless he could take a woman in his arms and comfort her. He stuck out his hand tentatively and patted her heaving shoulder.

"There, there, Margaret. I know how hard it is. Don't cry." Margaret raised her head and dabbed at her eyes with the corner of her apron. "But don't you think you're being a tiny bit selfish with Pat? You know Sketch promised her the horse. You can't do anything about her loving horses; her love for them is all mixed up with her love for Sketch. She idolized him, you know, and you can't destroy one without destroying the other. So why not let her have this colt? It's so weak that it can't hurt a flea. Even if it lives it'll never have the strength to buck an honest buck. Let her pour out her affection on him instead of eating her heart out with wanting to ride every horse she sees. You can't keep her off horses. It's only fair, Margaret. Let her have this one of her own."

"But, Doc, I can't. I'd hate it. I'd hate the very sight of it. Won't it always make friction between us?"

"Now you're talking like a child. If you make up your mind to be glad that the colt will make Pat happy, you know very well you can. You're not really a selfish woman, Margaret."

The woman sat still for a long while, biting her lip.

"You win, Doc. I guess I've been pampering myself in my troubles. She can have the colt and I give you my word I'll try not to interfere."

Doc leaned over and kissed her lightly on the forehead.

"I'm old enough to do that, Margaret. You know how much I care about you both."

Margaret flushed, she jumped up and ran to the stove where the coffee was boiling over. When she lifted it off she went to the door and called Pat. The girl dropped her sponge into the bucket—she had almost taken off the first coat of mud—and came hesitantly across the yard. In the doorway she looked anxiously from Doc to her mother.

"Get yourself a glass of milk, Pat, and have a cookie." The milk was in the well in a bucket let down into the cool water by a rope. She didn't want to get it until she had taken a good look at Doc's face and her mother's, but neither of them told her a thing. Doc wasn't even smiling. She took a glass from the cupboard and went out the kitchen door. It was scarcely a minute's work to pull up the milk bucket, fill her glass and pour a little into an old pie pan that belonged to Shep, the collie who was sniffing around her feet. As she carried the glass into the kitchen her hand trembled, so that the milk rocked as though it were being whipped by a wind.

Sliding to her place at the table, Pat looked from one to the other. They were talking about Ty's wanting to go to California and the rich Easterner who was dickering to buy his ranch. Doc might have given her a sign to tell her it was all right, or at least have shaken his head but he was looking at Margaret with that way he had of laughing with his eyes while he kept his face as solemn as a church. Pat thrust a cookie into her mouth but she couldn't swallow it. Little needles of suspense pricked her arms and legs and it was torture to sit still but she couldn't move, she didn't dare to, not until someone mentioned Harmony.

Doc brushed the crumbs from his moustache and said he'd best be going. Margaret smiled at him, a secret, almost happy smile that made Pat catch her breath.

"Thank you for coming, Doc. Thank you for so many things. Tell Ty it was very kind of him to give Pat the colt. It was too much for him to do."

"Oh, he's nothing to look at. Ty was for shooting him but Pat wanted him so badly that she snatched him right out from under the gun, so you needn't worry. He isn't any loss to Ty."

"Then you're going to let me keep him?" Pat knocked over her milk as she threw herself upon her mother. The glass crashed onto the floor, splintering into a dozen pieces.

"See what you've done." Margaret pushed the hair back from Pat's flaming cheeks. "Wipe up the milk and we'll go to the corral."

The colt was standing where Pat had left him. Most of the mud had been sponged off and his damp coat showed even more plainly the outlines of his skeleton. His hip bones looked sharp enough to punch holes in his skin.

"Is this a horse?" Margaret couldn't help laughing at the grotesque creature. Pat flushed.

"Wait and see what Pat and I will do with him." Doc had opened his valise and was taking out bottles and tubes, arranging them on the pile of wood by the gate of the corral. "Here's some carbolic acid salve and Vaseline; this tube's for his eyes. Don't use too much, and put a little of this antiseptic in the water you sponge with. You may find a lot of sores and scratches. And here's some liniment. I'll make a horse doctor out of you yet, my girl. Oats in the morning and warm mash at night beside what grass he'll eat. Don't force him. Don't try to break or train him until he gets a little strength. You know how to take care of a horse. I'll be over in a few days with some oats and bran. Call me up if you need me."

He closed the door of his pickup, backed out of the corral and waved to them when he started down the road. The car roared off. Pat turned toward her mother, wanting to thank her, but Margaret Cole's face had gone cold again.

"You'll have to clean a stall and throw down some hay. Don't forget to feed the chickens before supper." She went into the house without looking back and carefully shut the door.

Pat stood watching her, trying to choke back tears. Why did everything have to be wrong between them? It was getting late, the prairie was mottled with the shadows of its little hills. Pat carried Doc's medicines into the stable and arranged them on a shelf, then she began to clean out the box stall nearest the door. It was thick with dust, bits of rope, trash that had accumulated since the horses had gone away. When she had carpeted it with a bed of clean straw she brought in Harmony and gave him a bucket of fresh water that fitted into a boxed-in corner which Sketch had made for it. She took to the door an old horse blanket that no one had wanted to buy and gave it a good beating to get out the dust, then put it over Harmony.

"I guess you're good and dry now." She patted his shoulder and his sharp rump. "You'll like it here. There are some swallows in those nests on the rafters and they'll be company. And so is old Shep. You're going to like him. I've got to go and feed the chickens now." Harmony flicked one ear as though he was too tired to care.

In the kitchen, after supper, Margaret sewed while Pat washed the dishes. She was making Pat a summer dress, a cotton print with a tight bodice and a full peasant skirt, little sprigs of white flowers on a blue ground.

"Come here and let me measure. Don't you think it's pretty?"

"Yes," Pat answered with no enthusiasm.

"Sketch wouldn't like you to go around in jeans all the time."

Pat was standing close enough to Margaret to stroke her smooth hair.

"Mommie, you don't really hate Harmony, do you?"

"No, of course not. I don't love him the way you do but I'm glad you have him." She brushed her cheek against Pat's. "We'll have to stick together very close now that we haven't got Sketch."

"Oh, Mommie, Mommie, we will." She stood very still with her arm held out for her mother to measure, scarcely daring to breathe. Margaret had come back to her for the first time since Sketch had died.

When she went out to see how Harmony was getting along, the sun was setting. At the farthest western edge of the prairie the sky was striped with rose and gold, gentle colors that flowed into each other and gradually suffused the whole dome of the sky with a rosy glow. She wanted to show it to Harmony but he was already asleep, with his head drooping and his ears laid back, so she sat on the corral fence and watched it alone.

Shep lumbered up and rubbed his head against her leg. She was tired, so tired with all the things that had happened that her very bones ached. She slumped against a post and felt the rose light flow around her. All at once she knew that Sketch was sitting beside her on the fence, the heels of his cowboy boots hooked over the rail. He was looking across the prairie the way he used to, not saying a word until suddenly the darkness fell. Then he would say, "That's the most beautiful thing you'll ever see, honey." Pat didn't look at him, she just knew he was there and that he was telling her, "Everything will be all right, Patsy Pie." She didn't need to see him or hear the words. He was there and then he was gone, but she wouldn't think of him as dead any more, buried in the cemetery where she could never reach him. Now she knew that he would never be far away.

Chapter 3

The Snubbing Post

It was broad daylight when Pat awoke. She pulled on her jeans and sweater and ran out to look at the colt. He was still half asleep, but his eyes seemed better and he was steadier on his feet. She took off his blanket, put a halter over his head and led him into the corral, where he blinked weakly at the sun. If she hadn't been afraid of knocking him over she would have hugged him, her heart was so full of the glory of owning him. She was going to feed Harmony up until he was as sleek as Rajah, Sketch's parade horse, who wore the silver-mounted saddle. She would take him to the horse shows, as she and Sketch had planned, and he would win so many prizes that maybe they could go clear to New York and Madison Square Garden.

She imagined New York as a four-cornered game in which you pushed a red light and all the people on one end moved across to the other, and when you pushed a green light those on the side lines rushed across the field. It was something like prisoner's base or musical chairs. Those who got caught in the middle were "it." Madison Square Garden, a building large enough to hold bucking steers and broncos and cowgirls riding quadrilles on calico ponies, was too much for her imagination. She could see only Harmony standing proudly in a blaze of

light. As she patted him on his hollow rump, she heard the ex-
clamations from the crowd. "Why, she's only a little girl! How
can she ride so well!"

What she actually heard was her own voice saying to Harmony, "You stay here and warm up while I clean your stall."
Before she gave him his breakfast she had to feed the chickens.
Bowing her head slightly, as though she were acknowledging
the plaudits of the crowd, she dug a bucket into the grain bin
and carried it behind the barn, where the chickens were running loose; Margaret kept a scraggly lot for eggs. Pat tossed
the grain to them contemptuously. They had such gluttonous
ways, pushing and shoving, not a well-mannered one among
them. One fat gray hen ran into the thickest scattering of grain,
trying to gobble up the feed so quickly that she almost choked.
Pat laughed at her as she interrupted her frenzied pecking to
attack any chicken that came within reach of her beak. And
the turkeys were no better; they had such malicious red eyes.
It was all she could do to keep from running when a gobbler
strutted toward her. She filled the water trough and looked for
eggs, only six this morning. When she took them into the house,
Margaret called that breakfast was ready.

"Just a minute, Mummy." She ran back to the stable and
gave Harmony his oats. He followed her to the stall without
waiting to be led. "Shows how bright he is," she thought. "He
already knows where to find his breakfast."

"Sweetheart, eat your cereal. The colt won't run away," Margaret said. Pat bolted her breakfast, gulped down her milk and
threw her arms around her mother's neck with a wordless hug,
then dashed back to the stable where Harmony was taking his
time. When he had scooped up his last bite of oats she crosstied him and began his grooming. He would have stood without
the ropes, for he didn't have the strength to pull away, but Pat
wanted to do everything right, as Sketch would have done it.
This time when she sponged Harmony the last of the mud came

off and his rough, coarse hair showed a glowing chestnut. With one of Sketch's rubber currycombs, she brushed away at the matted hair that came out in wads. By the time she had brushed and polished him it was noon. She turned him into the hay meadow beside the creek, the best pasture on the ranch.

Through the long June days, Pat worked with her colt, looking him over every morning for scratches, putting ointment on the scabby places on his skin and grooming him until there wasn't a loose hair on his hide. By midsummer, when it was so hot that Harmony's flanks were dark from perspiration just from the rubbing, his coat began to take on a healthy glow and he was able to gallop across the pasture, but his hip bones were still sharp.

"Takes time to fill him out," Doc said, "but you're doing a good job, my girl. Don't try to ride him this summer. Let him get his strength. He's going to be a big horse and I shouldn't be surprised if he turns out to be a jumper." The colt was so dependent on Pat that he followed her about with the coquettish airs of a kitten, nuzzling her hand looking for carrots or sugar, rubbing his nose against her back.

"He's too old to act so babyish," Margaret said. "You'd think he was a foal instead of a two-year-old, but maybe he's making up for the time he lost." She neither petted the colt nor talked to him, but he had so little strength that she felt no antagonism toward him, no fear that he would harm Pat.

In the afternoons, Pat walked over to Ma Chisholm's even if it wasn't the day for the mail. Sometimes Jake let her ride one of the horses when he needed someone to help him round up the herd and bring them into the corral or drive them from one pasture to the other. When Doc was there, he usually came out to give her a leg up and see that she had the bridle reins between the proper fingers.

"When Harmony's strong enough you ought to ride bare-

back," he said. "It's good for the muscles. Teaches you how to
guide a horse without sawing on the bit."

Jake was working on the yearlings, breaking them to the
halter. He had such confidence in Pat that he let her help him
in the little round corral in which the snubbing post stood. He
even let her hold the end of the great loop of rope that he hung
on a piece of wire hooked over the top rail of the corral. When
he drove the colt through the loop, Pat jerked it tightly around
the animal's neck, then gave the rope to Jake while she darted
quickly out of the way of the colt's hoofs. When Jake had
wrapped the end of the rope around the post he let Pat hold it
again while he edged up to the colt, plunging on the end of the
rope, and tried to gentle him, holding out his hand to touch
the horse's face, ears and neck while the animal danced and
yanked, snorting with terror.

Jake was gentle and infinitely patient and as nimble as a cat
when it came to getting out of a colt's way. Once a colt had
kicked him on the knee and it had taken him a whole summer
to limber it up again. Now he wasn't taking chances. Every once
in a while he called to Pat to tighten the rope. Sometimes it
took him half an hour or longer to pull the colt up on a short
rope and get a halter over his head. Then he attached the snubbing rope to the halter, tied the colt to a post in the big corral
and left him there for two or three hours to learn that a rope
and halter were things from which there was no way of getting
free. Sometimes they worked with three or four colts in an afternoon. Pat wanted to try her hand at the gentling, but Jake
would never let her.

"If I get kicked it's my own hard luck," he said, "but I'm not
going to carry you back to your mother with a broken leg or
arm. She'd never let you look at another horse."

One afternoon when she and Jake were working on a particularly fractious colt, a beautiful coal-black filly with a white star

on her forehead, she noticed Ty leaning on the gate of the corral. With him was a man in riding breeches and a khaki shirt. His legs were encased in puttees and his boots didn't have high heels.

"Hi, cowboy," he called, waving to her. "Where did *you* come from?"

"Best little trainer in these parts," Jake said, wiping the damp hair out of his eyes.

The man unbarred the gate, came across and took the snubbing rope. He pulled it so tight that the black filly began to wheeze.

"Don't, don't. Let her out. You'll burn her neck with the rope," Pat cried, grabbing his arm. The man loosened the rope and held it for a while, then gave it back to her.

"You're better than I am." He stood aside and watched her, a slim mite with her jeans splotched with dust, her red checked blouse clinging wet to her back, her cheeks flushed and a curly blonde halo escaping from her pigtails.

"Let's keep her on," he called to Jake with a grin. "We can use a good hand."

The man and Ty walked away to the big corral where Jake and Pat had rounded up the horses. When she came into the kitchen he was talking to Doc and eating Ma's hot biscuits with honey on them. He got up, went into Jake's room, and came back with a box of candy—a store box with a bow of gold and silver ribbons on it.

"Here's your first pay," he said, giving it to Pat with a flourish. "What do you think of my new assistant, Ma?"

All the way home Pat carried the box carefully wrapped in her kerchief to keep it free from dust. Margaret was ironing when she came in and laid it on the table.

"You can have the first piece," Pat said. "The man from Kansas City gave it to me." But she didn't mention what he had said about her being a good cowhand. She untied the gilt and

silver ribbons and rolled them into two smooth balls, then
opened the box and held it out to Margaret. Chocolates, creams
and nuts and cherries with brandy inside. Once Sketch had
brought her such a box.

"Was that the man who wants to buy the ranch?" Margaret
asked. "What was he like?"

"Tall and sort of slick looking, as if he were currycombed
every day, and nice. He has a long blue car with the top rolled
back like Sketch's but he doesn't know much about breaking
horses." Pat chose a cream and took it out to Harmony. One
wouldn't hurt him. It was time for his supper; he told her so
by nuzzling her playfully toward the barn.

After supper, Margaret and Pat sat by the screen door, where
it made a draft with the open window, trying to catch what
breeze there was, watching the prairie fade from gold to rose
and gray. It was nine o'clock when the dark fell and Margaret
put on the light. Every time she pushed the button she thought
of Sketch. The wind charger, a sort of modern mechanical windmill that gave them electricity, was the only useful present
Sketch had given her. All the neighboring ranches had them,
but to Sketch such conveniences did not matter. He would have
given Margaret a beaver coat with much more pleasure than
electric light.

To Pat, the lights had no such associations. She liked to watch
the dim whitewashed walls jump out sharply, the curves of
the great logs throwing shadows that made gray stripes across
them. Her mother didn't pick up her sewing, she was thinking
about the man from Kansas City and wondering about Ty and
Ma. Nobody believed that Ty would actually sell his ranch. He
had been her father's best friend. They had come into this sec-
tion together when it was first opened in 1908, and had taken
up land next to each other. He had been almost as close to her
as her father. If Ty and Ma left she would feel utterly alone.
She went to the box phone on the wall and, twisting the handle,

gave the bell two long rings and a short. Maybe Gladys, Ty's married daughter who lived on a ranch this side of Bison, would know what was going on. She hated to ask Ty himself. He never liked to talk about his business.

Gladys had no news except what they all knew, that he was thinking about selling. She didn't know about the broker from Kansas City. While Margaret told her about Pat's encounter with the Easterner, Ma Chisholm's voice interrupted. It was a co-operative phone and practically everybody in the county was on the line. All the neighbors could listen in on a conversation or join in for that matter, and they usually did.

"Hello, Margaret," Ma said. "I heard someone ring Gladys and thought it might be you. Now you two girls stop worrying about Dad. He'll tell you all about it as soon as there's anything definite to tell. Margaret, Dad wants to see you. He has something on his mind. Could you come over tomorrow afternoon?"

The next morning while Pat combed and polished Harmony, Margaret ironed a dress for herself and one for Pat. After dinner she scrubbed Pat until her skin shone, braided her hair, tied the ends with blue ribbons, buttoned her into the new full-skirted dress and told her to sit by the table and keep still.

Pat watched Margaret dress. She liked to see her mother undo and brush her lustrous hair.

"I'll bet you could sit on it if you wanted to!" she said. Margaret wound her plaits and slipped on the freshly-ironed dress, with its rose-peppermint stripes. Sketch had brought her the material from Rapid City. "You're awfully pretty when you're dressed up. I wish you could stay that way all the time."

Margaret flushed with pleasure.

"You're not so bad looking yourself. I'd tell you what pretty eyes you have if it wouldn't make you vain. Come on now and don't get any grease on your dress."

Margaret tied kerchiefs about their heads and went out into the back yard to start the car. She had sold the Chrysler convertible that Sketch had given her. There were still payments due on it and she couldn't afford to keep it, so she had traded it for a secondhand Ford. It bucked ahead now over the prairie like a lame jack rabbit. Margaret had no feeling for machinery and she didn't drive well; she had never driven when Sketch was at home, but now that the horses were gone she was trying to master the Ford.

The blue car was in front of the Chisholm door, but the Easterner and Jake had gone to ride the fences.

"Wants to see what he's getting," Ty said as he sat across from Margaret at the table.

"You needn't tell me this child had chocolate angel cake for dessert." Ma was bringing in handsome wedges of it with coffee, and a glass of milk for Pat.

"No, since we were coming over here I starved her on purpose. And me too. Ma, I don't know how I'm going to stand it if you and Ty go away."

"Now, don't you get upset, my dear. We aren't gone yet." Ty had agreed to stay for one year, he told her, and manage the ranch for Mr. Lennox who was going to send up a trainer in the spring. He planned to train his horses here before he took them East. Then Ty and Ma were going to California. Ty hadn't said much about it, but his bad leg had been troubling him more than ever lately and he hadn't been able to help Jake as he should. It took at least two able-bodied men to run the place. With his parents gone, Jake could marry Lily Stiles, whose father was getting old too and wanted him to run their ranch; it would be too much for him to carry on the two places.

Margaret's eyes filled with tears.

"It will be almost as hard as losing Dad."

Ma poured her another cup of coffee.

"Don't say such morbid things. Being dead is a lot different from being in California. Tell her what you wanted to see her about, Dad."

Ty lifted his eyebrows, which were as thick as tumbleweed and made black smudges under his bristling white hair. His massive face creased broadwise which meant, Pat knew, that he was going to take a crack at Ma. Ever since she could remember his face had fascinated her. When he made a joke his cheeks folded up like an accordion from ear to ear and when he was horse trading or talking about business, they hung down like the jowls of his prize bull.

"Just shows you women don't always get your gossip straight." He told Margaret they had all been wrong about the teacher of the Snake Creek School. Miss Nancy was going to get married after all; she'd made up with the rancher on Elk Horn who'd been courting her for years. As president of the school board, Ty offered the job to Margaret.

"You went to normal school before Sketch roped you," he said, "and you could brush up enough to do it."

"Mummy teach me!" Pat stopped licking chocolate from her fingers and stared at Ty in consternation. She was the oldest of the eight pupils in the school and their leader. Miss Nancy always had depended upon her. "Patty, will you stick the witches on the windows for Halloween?" and "Patty, will you cut out these pictures of the three wise men and the shepherds?" Her mother wouldn't show her any favors. But Margaret was so pleased that it was no use to say a word.

"Then, it's all right," Ty was saying. "Turn your sheep in with Ed Lancaster's. He won't charge you much to look after them and he can graze them on both your ranges. You couldn't take care of them in the winter anyway."

Pat didn't want to listen, she had too much to think about. Slipping out of her chair, she ran into the yard to look for Jake, but there was no one around the corral. She saw his carryall rolling across the south pasture and ran to meet it. Mr. Lennox was with him and they had a shotgun between them.

"Shiver my timbers if it isn't our cowhand all dressed up. Hop in." Mr. Lennox made room for Pat between him and the gun. As they rattled into the yard, Ty and Ma and Margaret were standing beside the Ford. Mr. Lennox helped Pat out as though she were eighteen. Ty was introducing him to Margaret.

"You see, I already know your daughter. She's the best little horse trainer I ever saw and I'm thinking of taking her on as my straw boss."

Pat gasped. It was on the tip of her tongue to say, "I never did a thing but hold the snubbing rope for Jake," but her mother wasn't angry. Her eyes were smiling and her head bent toward Mr. Lennox, but Pat didn't think she was paying attention to a word he said.

Chapter 4

The Party

When Pat went out to feed the chickens the wind nearly blew her off her feet. Harmony, whom she had let out into the corral, stood with his head close against the lee side of the barn. When Pat scattered the feed it blew so far that the old gray hen ran after it in a frenzy, clucking and beating off competitors with her wings. Tossing the rest of it low on the ground, she backed toward the house; her eyes and mouth full of dust and her hair whipping her face. There was something lawless about the wind; it was a roistering stranger from no one knows where, a little drunk, whacking everybody as it passed. Scurrying to the kitchen, Pat felt her heart pounding with excitement.

Inside she was safe but the exhilaration was gone; she felt as deflated as a blownup paper bag that a child had popped. As she sponged the dust from her eyes at the shelf under the kitchen window she saw Margaret coming from the barn with the morning's milk, her head bent, pushing against the wind. Pat opened the door for her mother and leaned on it to close it. The milk was covered with a scum of dust as though someone had peppered it with cinnamon. When she had strained it through a clean cloth, Margaret poured a glass for Pat and dished up a saucer of oatmeal from a pot on the back of the stove.

"We're almost out of flour," she said. "I must go to town for some groceries. It's going to be a scorching day. Will you watch the bread and put it in the oven when it has risen enough?" She poured herself a cup of coffee and tossed a biscuit to Shep, who was pressing his nose against the screen.

As soon as her mother was off, Pat ran out to the soddy. Margaret had said she might have half of it for her tackroom. On one side, Pat had arranged her saddle soap and the medicine that Doc had given her. An old sawhorse that she had found in the barn made a good rest for the saddle, and the bridle she had hung on a peg on the wall.

Pat loved the soddy. Her grandfather had built it single-handed. He had cut the lush, thickly-rooted sod, by the creek, in strips three feet wide; these he cut in two-foot slabs and laid them like brick, one row overlapping the other. He had used no uprights, not a piece of wood anywhere except for window and door frames and the split logs for the roof. Now the building sagged a little. Every year or two Margaret had persuaded Sketch to plaster the chinks with mud. Once he had cemented the sides of the opening in which the door frame stood (it was three feet deep and rounded at the outer edge) and had scratched in it all the cattle brands he knew. The dirt floor on which Margaret had played as a baby was hard and clean. Pat kept it swept and the shelves dusted as though it were her own house.

Today she was going to undo all the buckles of her bridle and give it and the saddle a good soaping to keep the leather pliable. Sketch used to do it every day when he was riding, but Pat tried to do it once a week. Then she wanted to groom Harmony.

She took a bucket to the well to draw water for her spong-

ing. The wind had gone down a little and was only playing
with the buffalo grass. Harmony had left the shelter of the
barn and was standing by the corral gate watching her as
Shep ran after her, getting under her feet. She threw a chip at
the dog. He carried it back to her, not quite near enough for
her to get it, cavorting as though he were a puppy. He hadn't
played this game for so long that Pat thought he had forgotten
it. She chased him and retrieved the chip. He barked, wagging
his tail in a happy frenzy. Harmony whinnied impatiently, flicking first one ear, then the other. When Pat pushed her hair
out of her face to see what he wanted, he stood with his head
bent, his nose pushing against the gate.

"What's he doing?" she thought. "He can't be working at
the bar. He's not smart enough." She threw the chip to Shep
again and watched the colt out of the corner of her eye. The
bar fell to the ground with a thud. Harmony nosed the gate
open and pranced into the yard. Shep leaped about him snap-
ping at his tail, and Harmony kicked out with his back heels,
careful not to touch the dog. Pat ran after them, bursting with
pride. She had to tell somebody. If Bob Lancaster, the boy on
the neighboring ranch, was at home he would think she was
telling fairy tales. She left the dog and horse playing tag with
each other and went into the house. Two long and two short.
She took down the receiver but someone was on the line; Bob's
mother was telling a cousin that one of the cows was very sick,
nearly died during the night. Doc was there giving her calcium.
When Mrs. Lancaster stopped for breath, Pat broke in.

"This is Pat Cole, Mrs. Lancaster. I'm terribly sorry about
the cow. I've been trying to get Doc. I wonder if you'll ask him
to stop here when he comes this way."

Mrs. Lancaster said she would, and Pat hung up, not wanting to hear more about the cow. She took the white cloth off the
bread and looked at it. Just right to put into the pans. She
squeezed the dough into three big loaves, filled two pans with

rolls, stuck the loaves into the oven, made up the fire and then hurried back to the yard. She wanted Harmony to look his best for Doc.

But Harmony had no intention of being groomed. He wanted to play; every time Pat came near enough to catch him, he snorted as though he were laughing at her and backed away. "Why you great big devil," she called after him. "You think you're strong enough to get away from me." Harmony nickered and wheeled on Shep, sending him flying across the yard. Pat went to the barn and brought out a light snubbing rope. For half an hour she and Harmony circled each other. He could have escaped if he had wanted to for there was no fence nearer than the creek, but he didn't want to get away; he was frolicking with Pat. When she finally managed to throw the noose around his neck he did not pull away, but waited for her to come up to him and then nuzzled her hand.

She took him to the barn, crosstied him and set to work, washing the dust from his eyes and nose, brushing him, polishing him until his coat glowed.

"Now stay here till Doc comes," she said, closing the door of his box stall, "and no tricks till he gets here."

She hurried back to the house to see about the bread. It was just done. She rubbed a little butter on the golden-brown tops and set the loaves to cool, then popped in the rolls. Maybe Doc would come before dinner. She never had cooked a dinner by herself but she could. She would have hot rolls—Doc liked them with buffalo berry jam—half a chicken, left from the day before, that she would warm in the frying pan, potatoes, she knew how to mash them until they looked like cream, and a can of her mother's beans from the soddy. There was still part of a chocolate cake in the breadbox, and coffee—anyone could make coffee. She set the table with her mother's linen cloth with the little cross-stitch birds on it and the wedding ring china that Grandma had brought from Pennsylvania. There

were only three good plates left and Margaret never used
them, but this was a special occasion: Pat's first guest and her
first dinner. She put on the potatoes. He would come just as she
took the rolls out of the oven; this was one of those days when
everything was going to turn out right.

And it did. Just before she took out the rolls she looked
through the window and saw Doc's car a long way off across
the prairie. By the time she had buttered the rolls he was driving up to the kitchen door. She waved to him with a piece of
buttered paper.

"Here I am," he said, standing in the doorway and knocking
the dust from his hat. "Anything wrong with Harmony?"

"Nothing's wrong but something happened and I just had to
tell you because you're the only one who will believe it." She
poured Doc a bowl of water and while he washed his face and
hands told him about Harmony undoing the bolt.

"Of course, I believe it. I once had a colt that learned to open
the kitchen door and ask for a biscuit. Once he came right
through the kitchen into the living room, while my mother was
having one of her church guilds to tea. You should have heard
the commotion. After that she kept the door latched inside.
Um, um, what do I smell? Hot rolls?"

"Yes, we're having a party. Mummy's gone to town and I'm
cooking a dinner for you. My first party. Then I thought I'd
show you my tackroom in the soddy, fixed up just the way you
said, and maybe we could get Harmony to open the gate again."

Pat kept her eyes on the stove. It took a wizard to mash the
potatoes, watch the chicken browning and take up the beans,
all at the same moment. The table looked festive with the best
plates and a few blue morning glories in a white bowl. Pat
minded her manners and didn't forget to pass the butter or to
ask Doc if he would have a second helping.

Doc told her about his horses and hounds when he was young

on a plantation in eastern Virginia; how he and the others rode
to hounds on frosty October and November afternoons, jumping stone walls, farm gates and ditches, sometimes with the fox
laughing at them for all their trouble. Then they would come
home in the dusk, bone cold, to a fire and a hot rum punch. He
told her about a rangy old gray horse, a hunter who was so
good that when he caught diphtheria his owner refused to have
him shot. Doc operated on him and stuck a little tube through
his neck into his windpipe and there it stayed, only needing to
be cleaned out once in awhile. When the horse was in his stride
you could hear the wind whistling through the tube. And he
told her about the greatest hunter in his county whom someone
discovered pulling a garbage cart. He took all kinds of honors
but could never get rid of the marks of the collar on his neck.

"You'd like to ride to hounds, Pat. I'm sorry there's no hunting in this country but we can teach Harmony to jump and
you can ride in the shows. Next spring when he is as well and
strong as he'll ever be, we'll set up some jumps for him."

Pat didn't hurry Doc over the cake and coffee, and he lingered
for a second cup. At last he brushed his napkin over his moustache.

"You're the first young lady who's invited me to dinner for
a long, long time and I've never tasted a better one." Pat
glowed.

"Come and see the soddy," she said eagerly.

Standing in the doorway Doc looked at the cattle brands on
the cement.

"You know, I've never been inside. Your grandfather had
built the log house before I came. These soddies must have been
comfortable: cool in the summer, warm in winter. Most of
them are gone now, their roofs caved in, their walls just a heap
of dirt." He glanced at Margaret's shelves with their neat rows
of bags and jars, then at Pat's gear. He ran his hand over the

saddle and felt the bridle leather to see how supple she had kept it. The bit and the metal buckles of the bridle gleamed and it was as clean as if it had just come from a harness shop.

"I mustn't forget I have something for you in the car." Doc went out and rummaged in the back of the pickup and produced a rubber bit.

"We'll put this in the bridle. Harmony's well enough to break to the bridle now and this bit won't hurt him as much as the metal one, until he gets used to it. Put the bridle on him when you turn him out and let him wear it an hour or so a day. Then in about a week when he becomes accustomed to the bridle, you might begin to work him on the long reins. You probably haven't any leather ones, but pieces of old clothesline will do. If you haven't any, I'll find some. Time you began to train him how to move straight and answer to the rein."

He looked at the jars and boxes carefully aligned on the shelf and added to them a roll of bandage and some court plaster.

"How does the salve work? Has he gotten many scratches on the barbed wire?"

"Only a little one and I cured that. There isn't any scar. He hasn't a single blemish."

"Do tell." Doc forgot his party manner and twisted one of Pat's braids. "Getting sort o' proud, aren't you? Let's see the perfect creature."

They went across to the barn where Harmony, tired of being shut in, was kicking at the sides of his stall. Pat slipped a halter on him and led him into the corral. As he came through the door, a little brown creature, not much bigger than a rat, scuttered out of the barn.

"Why, it's a puppy. Where did he come from?" Pat dropped the halter and advanced toward the dog slowly to avoid frightening it, holding out her hand. The puppy crawled toward her on his belly, his whole body quivering with friendliness. She picked him up and the tiny fox-pointed face, with a white spot on it, looked eagerly up at her. His coat was chestnut, just the shade of Harmony's.

"What kind is he, Doc?"

"Blessed if I know, but with that face I'd say he has a touch of coyote. Nice, well-developed little fellow. Must have wandered away from a drifting cowpoke."

Pat held him out to Harmony, who first sniffed then fondled the puppy with his nose. The pup liked it, he began to lick Harmony on the face.

"Tip, I'll call him for his little sharp-pointed ears. Oh, Doc, I hope he stays. I'll get him some milk."

While Pat brought out a saucer of milk, Doc went over Harmony carefully, examining his face, his ears, his nostrils, his back and legs. Pat was right, there wasn't a scar on him. His ribs still showed and his hip bones, but his coat was sleek and he held his head up. He looked alive.

"Guess you're right, Pat. I can't find anything wrong with him."

Pat set down the milk and the puppy lapped it up. When the pup had finished, Harmony lowered his head gently and inched his nose toward the little fellow. Tip rolled forward on his stomach until they were scarcely a dozen inches apart; he lay there sprawled on his belly, legs spread out, tail beating the dust in an attitude of abject and, at the same time, coquettish adoration.

"I wish Harmony'd open the gate again. Shall we try?" Pat asked. "Let's go out into the yard and I'll call Shep." Outside, with the bolt set in the corral gate, Pat whistled for Shep. He came lazily from the shade behind the barn. Pat threw him a chip but Shep looked at it indifferently. The wind had died, it was hot and the elation of the morning was gone.

"Come, Shep, don't be lazy." Pat threw the chip again and ran after it herself. Shep came along at her heels as though it were his duty, but he didn't want to play. Very well, if he wouldn't, he wouldn't. She tossed up the chip and chased it, shouting and flapping her arms, giving the best imitation she could of an exciting game, meanwhile watching Harmony.

Doc laughed until his spectacles fell off.

"No go," he spluttered. "You can't fool Harmony. He's having a better time with the pup."

Pat stopped gyrating and sailed the chip away as far as she could throw it.

"That's an idea. Let's bring the puppy out and play with him." She ran to the corral, picked up the dog and fastened the gate ostentatiously behind her. Setting the pup on the ground, in full view of Harmony, she began to pet it, rolling it over on its back, rubbing its fat stomach, then stepping off a pace or two, she encouraged it to come to her.

Harmony came to the gate and looked over anxiously; then he raised his head and nickered. When Pat paid him no attention he snorted and butted at the gate. It didn't give.

"Look, Doc, look," Pat called, dancing with excitement. "He's doing it." Harmony had lowered his head and was pushing at the bar. This time he went at it as though he knew what he was about. Doc took out his big gold hunting watch. In less than five minutes Harmony pushed out the bolt, butted the gate open and trotted into the yard. He nuzzled Pat's shoulder, then put his nose on the ground waiting for the pup to lick it.

Pat rubbed Harmony's neck and looked across at Doc, her eyes burning with pride.

"Yes, he's a smart horse, and we'll win some prizes with him if we work hard enough. Meanwhile, you ought to be riding, Pat. Go over and help Jake every chance you get."

Doc went to the car and climbed in.

"Thank you for a delicious dinner. And, Pat, let the dog stay in the stall with Harmony. He won't hurt it. I once had a horse who fell in love with a goat. When that goat was around, the horse was the best hunter I ever had; but when it wasn't, he went into a decline. After awhile I got a collar for the goat and chained it to the stall. Not that you need to do that with this pup. He'll stay. You'll see; they'll play together. Humor Harmony when what he wants won't hurt him. There never was a good horse that wasn't temperamental." He honked good-by.

Pat watched him drive out of sight, then turned Harmony and the pup into the hay meadow. She hadn't soaped her bridle, but there were the dishes to do before Margaret came home. Filling a dishpan with hot water, she sloshed her hands in it to the rhythm of a song Sketch used to sing when Pat was little and he rode her on his foot.

> *And when I die, don't bury me at all,*
> *Just pickle my bones in alcohol.*

It had never made sense to her, but Sketch used to roar with laughter when she repeated it after him. She shouted it at the top of her high, clear voice because she was so happy she had to sing.

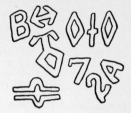

Chapter 5

The First Rail

The next time Doc came by, Pat and Harmony were in the field behind the barn and did not see him drive up. Hearing the joyous yapping of Tip, he walked across to the corral and stood in the shadow of the gate watching them. It was still early and a cool breeze from across the buttes had not yet been stifled by the August heat. It rippled over the grass, the clumps of pink thistles beyond the sheds and ripening tumbleweed and made the whole prairie seem alive. He took off his hat and felt the breeze pass through his hair. "What a country," he thought, feeling the magic that it had held for him when he first saw it forty years earlier. Pat, the colt and the dog playing in the meadow seemed to have grown out of the prairie like the wild broom and the yarrow.

Pat had laid a rail across a couple of low boxes not more than a foot above the ground and was leading Harmony over it with a strap and halter. He came easily, lifting each foot clear. Tip ran yelping and leaping after him. Pat threw her arms around Harmony's neck and gave him a lump of sugar.

Doc walked over to the colt, took hold of his halter and patted his neck.

[44]

"Now see if he'll jump." Doc took off the halter. "You jump and see if he'll follow you."

Pat jumped and looked back calling to Harmony. The colt edged up to the rail but he didn't jump, he sniffed it and hesitated. Pat ran around to his side, patted him reassuringly and jumped again. Harmony whinnied after her, stepped back, lifted his front feet, tucked them under his belly and cleared the jump with a good margin. Doc beamed.

"He folds beautifully. Pat, I think we have a born jumper. Let's raise the rail a bit. We could stand these boxes on end. That'll give us about a foot and a half."

Doc upended the boxes, replaced the rail, then laid two others from the boxes to the ground, sticking them out at an angle like partly-opened wings.

"We want him to start right," he explained, "and not get in the habit of running out. Now you take it. Can you?"

Pat made a little run and cleared the rail in a wide arc. Doc cheered.

"You have pretty good form yourself. Now call Harmony." The colt ran up to the rail, his mane flying, but he didn't jump, he eyed it curiously and stuck his nose over it, asking for sugar.

"No, no." Pat pushed him back, trying not to laugh at him. "You're just showing off. No jump, no sugar. Come on, see how I do it." She came around and jumped again. This time Harmony followed easily.

"He isn't afraid, he's just playing," Doc said. "I believe he could do three feet this minute. I wonder how he'd take a broader jump." He went into the barn and dragged out three bales of hay which he laid on the flat side, making a jump about two feet high and as wide. Pat tried it and although it was not as easy as the rail, she managed to get over without touching it.

The colt skimmed over the bale without hesitation.

"Not so good at the broad jump, eh. Well, we're not training you for an Olympic champion. Now call Harmony."

The colt sauntered up to the bale, folded his hoofs neatly under him and skimmed over it without a moment's hesitation.

"That's interesting," Doc commented. "He didn't mind this half as much as he did the light under the rail." He suggested that they take the jump three or four more times so Harmony wouldn't forget. Doc watched the colt's action and looked at his gleaming coat.

After a workout of about half an hour, Pat rubbed Harmony down and turned him loose in the pasture. Seeing that they were still watching him, he kicked up his heels and charged Tip with quick ferocious rushes. Tip yelped and snapped joyfully at his heels.

"I never dreamed he'd come back so quickly. It's hard to re-

member that weak-kneed, lead-eyed, mud-spattered creature
we brought home. You're doing a good job, Pat. His coat shines
as though you'd been feeding him linseed meal. Seems to me
we'd best act fast now and break him before he gets too frisky.
I know he follows you around like a pup, but he's got a lot of
power and we'd better teach him fast. How did the bridle go?
Do you put it on every day and let him tongue the bit?"

Pat nodded.

"I've even let him graze a little with it on and I've been driving him on the long lines. He goes pretty well," she said.

Then they'd begin with the saddle, Doc said, but not today.
Harmony had done enough. And he made Pat promise not to
attempt to ride him by herself. In a few days he would come
by this way and they'd put on the saddle.

"You'll be riding him in no time at all," he promised, tweak-
ing her braid. It would be pretty lonesome training him without any help, he said, but in the fall or certainly next spring
she'd see some real jumping. Mr. Lennox expected to bring
his show horses to the ranch when the horse shows were over,
and in the spring his trainer was coming. Between them, Doc
promised, they'd teach Pat all there was to know.

"Did his horses ever win any ribbons? Did they ever show
in Madison Square Garden or the American Royal?" Pat
asked.

"Both," Doc answered, laughing at her eagerness. "One of
them is a champion, has won all over the Middle West, a pretty
mare about the color of Harmony."

"Oh," Pat sighed, "I wish they'd come soon."

For a week, Pat worked Harmony every morning, drove him
with the long reins and took him over the jumps until they
both were bored with the same old lessons. The colt was like a
bright child whom the teacher has to keep amused. He did his
lessons with such ease that he was constantly looking for diver-

sions, running after Tip, refusing, tossing his head playfully as though he were laughing at Pat, only to take the jump the next time with faultless precision. She raised the rail to two and a half feet; that was as high as she herself could jump.

Every day she watched for Doc and he didn't come. She wanted to telephone him but knew that wouldn't be fair, he might have a lot of sick cattle on his hands. In desperation she wondered if Jake would help her with the saddle.

One morning after giving Harmony his workout, Pat went into the barn and sat on an upturned bucket idly watching the long horsetail hairs dangling from a swallow's nest on the beams. She could put the saddle on Harmony herself by cross-tying him, but she had promised Doc and she knew that Margaret would never forgive her. She had saddled her pony ever since she was tall enough to stand on a box and reach him. To be sure, she never had saddled an unbroken colt, but Harmony wouldn't hurt her.

This morning she didn't feel like soaping her saddle and bridle which were already spotless. It wasn't much fun working alone. If Sketch were here they'd be riding over to see Ty or exercising his cow ponies or practicing on the small herd of cattle that had belonged to Margaret's father. Sketch always had entered the cutting competitions at the rodeos and even on her pony his daughter had learned how to round up stragglers. Every day with Sketch had been full of excitement. Now there was nothing to do, nothing at all until she could ride Harmony. Even her daydreams failed her. She wanted to ride now, this very day. She wanted to race along a dirt road, feeling the wind in her eyes and the warm ribs of the horse against her knees. Without waiting to wash her hands, she started off across the prairie to Ty's. Maybe Jake would be at home and let her ride.

The weather was still and hot, a dry withering August heat

that shriveled your skin and sucked all the moisture out of your bones. The distance had never seemed so great. Nobody was in the house, not even Ma. Pat saw a crowd of people by the corrals and ran down to discover what was going on. Jake, Ty and Ma were there and a couple of men whom Pat didn't know. They were unloading a long van full of cattle: Black Angus, heavy, majestic, square-faced, stolid, with several frightened calves among them.

Ma saw Pat and called to her. They stood outside the corral and watched the men herd the cattle into the small corral that had the branding chute in it. Mr. Lennox had bought these cattle at the auction in Belle Fourche. He hoped they would help support his horses, Ma said. Jake noticed Pat and waved. He and one of the strangers were urging a black steer into the chute. The beast went unwillingly, driven between the high fences that narrowed at the end until the chute was no wider than the animal. One of the men thrust a rod across from fence to fence, close behind the steer to keep him from backing while the other let down the bar that held his head in a vise. Ty heated the branding iron in a shallow, open gasoline stove that made a flame like a blowtorch. He thrust it against the steer's side. It jumped and squirmed, but the vise held. The pungent odor of scorched fur assailed Pat's nostrils. She watched the welt rise where the brand had seared the hide. Ty took the running iron and deepened one of the letters of the brand. Jake raised the rod that held down the steer's head and opened the gate. The steer shot into the large corral and as soon as he saw that no one was molesting him, quieted down. Pat marveled that he did not seem in pain.

Next, a calf was driven into the chute. He was so small that the fences did not hold him tight. Jake took out the top board of the vise so it would be the right height for the calf's head and lowered the bar a notch or two. The calf plunged and fought.

Pat looked away to keep from seeing the terror in the bulging eyes. Ty had a hard time getting the iron pressed firmly against the animal's twitching side. The calf, too, bounced into the large corral and in a few minutes seemed to forget all about his fright.

"This is enough," Ma said to Pat. "Let's don't stand here any longer in the sun." The two walked back to the kitchen where Ma collapsed in her rocking chair and reached for her palm leaf fan.

"They're bringing two more loads. I guess they'll be out in that sun all afternoon." Ma wiped her forehead. "How would you like to take a nice cool shower and then we'll make some ice cream for supper. Afterward Jake's going over to Strool and he'll ride you home. I'll phone Margaret."

Pat grinned at Ma. How did she guess that Pat had wanted to take a bath in that wonderful green-tiled bathroom ever since it had been put in a year earlier? Ty had built a little ell for it between Ma's room and Jake's; it had not only a tub, but also a shower with a flowered curtain around it. Jake had said he had taken so many showers in the navy that he couldn't consider any other kind of bath.

Ma had intended to invite Pat to take a shower for a long time, but there always seemed to be so many people around.

"Get along now and try the green soap that Mr. Lennox brought. It's supposed to smell like pine needles." Ma shooed Pat toward her room and settled back in the rocker to take a nap. Pat latched the bathroom door, slipped off her jeans and blouse and stood with her bare feet on the cool white tiles. That, for the moment, was pleasure enough. Then she tiptoed to the shower and stepped in, pulling the curtain behind her. She looked at the gleaming chromium handles and the gooseneck that curved over her head. She twisted the handle marked "cold" and the water pelted down on her, stinging her skin like hail. She couldn't see or breathe. Exquisite shivers ran up and down her spine. Gasping, she reached blindly for the handle and turned it off. This was fun, as much fun as galloping on a frisky horse with the wind in your face. After she caught her breath she experimented, turning the water on slowly in a gentle spray, then full force until she had to stick her head out to breathe.

Presently she heard Ma calling, "Are you drowned?"

"I'm coming," she answered, and stepped out on the bathroom floor. Ma had told her to get a towel from the linen closet but she was shy about using other people's things so she walked around, flapping herself until she was dry enough to climb into her jeans. When she won her prize money she would get her mother a bathroom with tiles and chromium knobs and a little place built in the wall to hold the soap. Looking about to see that she had left everything neat, she flew into the kitchen to Ma.

"Don't hug me, you little wet mouse. Here, crack a few of these walnuts to put in the ice cream."

After supper, Jake got out his sedan that had been freshly washed. That meant he was going to see Lily Stiles. He said he would drop Pat home first. As she climbed in she planned to ask him to help her with Harmony, but when he was dressed up he seemed so old and important that she hadn't found courage to ask him before they pulled up at her door.

"I won't stop in to see Margaret," he said. "You tell her 'hello' for me. Good-by, honey. I'm coming over one day soon to see how you are making out with Harmony."

Before Pat could answer, Jake was off. She ran into the house bursting with news. After all, it had turned out to be a wonderful day.

"Mr. Lennox is getting lots of Black Angus," she told her mother, "and I watched Ty brand them. And Ma let me take a shower bath and it was gorgeous. Someday I'm going to get you a bathroom, Mummy, only you'd rather have a pink one, wouldn't you?"

"That would be nice," Margaret answered absently as she pared a potato.

Pat went out to give Harmony his supper. She *was* going to get her mother a pink-tiled bath and it *had* been a wonderful day. She would tell Harmony about it. He and Tip seemed to understand better than Margaret.

When she had thrown fresh straw from the loft and bedded down the colt for the night, she came back into the house and quietly washed her hands and face.

"I guess I'll go to bed, Mummy. I'm sort o' tired." Margaret kissed her absently.

"Good night, sweet."

But Pat did not undress immediately, she sat before her grandmother's old walnut dresser and undid her pigtails, still damp from the shower. It was a friendly room and she liked to look at it before she turned out the light. She liked the pink-plastered log walls and the rag rug that Granny had made for her. In the morning, when she wakened, she could lie in bed and see the corrals through the window, and farther away, the prairie rising in gentle swells to the fortress walls of the buttes with their crown of pines.

Finally Pat slipped between the sheets and closed her eyes with a contented sigh, imagining Harmony sailing over a gate, the two of them as one, she leaning forward almost on his neck, lifting him, feeling his muscles stretch. She had never seen jumping, but Doc had told her how it felt, like being lifted up by a wave—she could only imagine what that would be like—or riding on the wings of an eagle.

Chapter 6

The Magic of Sitting Bull

In the morning Doc came. Pat had known he would be there when she wakened early and ran out to give Harmony a work-out over the bar. She hurried to feed the chickens and fill the kitchen water bucket, singing at the top of her voice.

Margaret looked up from her dishpan and her voice fell like a cool spray on Pat's high spirits.

"Your breakfast is ready. Wash your face and brush the straw out of your hair." She set Pat's bowl of oatmeal at her plate and poured a glass of milk. After she had straightened up the house she was going to Bison to see the county superintendent about the opening of school, which was only a month away.

Pat said she'd rather stay at home, she thought Doc was coming by to help her train Harmony, and wished she hadn't said it when she saw the cloud on Margaret's face.

"If he doesn't come, will you promise not to try to put the saddle on the colt?" So, Margaret hadn't been indifferent, she knew how Harmony had progressed. Pat felt a glow of warmth around her heart.

"Of course, I'll promise, but I know he'll come."

And he did before Margaret left. He was driving to the buttes

to see a sick horse at a ranch some thirty miles away and thought
Pat might like to come with him. Margaret offered to make
them a picnic lunch. He insisted that they would have dinner
at the ranch, but when she took a fresh devil's food cake out of
the box, he weakened and let her fix them sandwiches and a
thermos of coffee. Margaret was glad to see Doc, but there was
an air of restrained disapproval about her.

When they waved Margaret good-by, Pat asked breathlessly
if they'd have time to put the saddle on Harmony.

"I've taught him everything you said and I've been watching for you every day."

Doc took off his tie and turned down the neck of his fresh
khaki shirt.

"I hope His Highness isn't feeling his oats."

Pat ran ahead to the pasture behind the barn. Harmony
wasn't far away but when she called he arched his neck and
pawed the grass as though he dared her to come and get him.
He didn't move until she could almost touch the halter which
she had left on, so sure was she that Doc would come. With it
almost within reach of her hand, Harmony side-stepped as
lightly as a ballet dancer, then tossed his head and ran a circle
around Pat. He stopped and waited for her to catch up with
him, then repeated the maneuver, dancing this time to the left
and circling in the other direction. "It's like a figure in a quadrille," Doc thought watching. "I swear that colt was born with
a sense of form. Somewhere on his family tree there must have
been a high-school horse."

When Harmony had teased Pat for a little, he did not wait
for her to catch the halter, but trotted before her into the corral.
Pat was hot and panting.

"Isn't he acting like a devil! Why didn't you help me?"

"Because you were putting on such a good show. That horse
is a born actor."

They took Harmony into his stall and crosstied him. Doc

brought the saddle from Pat's tackroom in the soddy and after working around Harmony for a while, leaning against him and stroking him, he gently shoved the saddle across the colt's back. Harmony didn't object, but when Doc tried to tighten the girth he lashed out with his back hoofs and went into a series of bucks, hunching his back and leaping into the air with his feet together, trying to bump it off. The saddle slid under his body but the girth buckle held.

Waiting a few minutes, Doc pulled the saddle back in place and tightened the girth a little farther. Harmony bucked again and tried to rub the saddle off against the side of his stall. He yanked on the ropes that held him and kicked his walls, but Doc was too near his head for the horse to reach him with his heels.

Presently Harmony calmed down and took a lump of sugar from Pat's hand. Tip slid into the stall and yapped at him, asking what it was all about. The colt leaned over and touched his partner with his nose.

"Talk to him gently, Pat. He isn't frightened, he's just annoyed. That's the worst of it." Doc edged out of the stall. "Always be careful to keep away from his heels. But you know that. I have the stirrups tied up and I'd leave them that way for the first few times, then let them dangle until they don't bother him. When he gets used to the saddle, lean your weight on it and every once in a while throw your arms over it. Then we'll tie a sack of grain on it and teach him to carry weight. But you can't lift a hundred-pound sack. Promise me you won't be silly enough to try. Either Jake or I will be around."

"Of course, I won't. When do you think I can ride him?"

"A couple of weeks, maybe. We'll leave him in the corral. We won't be gone long."

Harmony made no objection when Doc backed him out of the stall. He even let Pat stroke his neck. Doc took along a piece of wire that was hanging on the wall.

"We'd better fasten the gate. We don't want him opening it and wandering all over the buttes with the saddle."

As they twisted the wire around the gate post, Harmony eyed them sadly, then began to prance, buck and twist like a bronco.

"Doesn't want to be left. I never saw such a fellow. He's perfectly happy as long as he has an audience."

"But isn't he handsome? Don't you think he has a beautiful coat?"

"And a beautiful rider too, honey. We'll knock their eyes out in Kansas City. Sketch will be proud of you."

Pat looked up quickly. Doc, too, realized that Sketch hadn't gone away to some frightening other world, that he was right here on the ranch and knew what was happening to them.

They packed the sandwiches in the back of the pickup. The lunch caused Doc to think about Margaret. As they drove across the pasture and turned into a faint track that led toward the buttes, he asked, "Did I imagine that your mother isn't too pleased with us?"

Pat nodded.

"She won't tell me not to break Harmony, but she makes me feel as though I was doing something wrong all the time. As if I were being disloyal to her somehow."

"You poor child." Doc clutched the wheel as the car bumped into the end of a narrow, half-hidden wash. "You've got to try to understand your mother, but forget about it now. Let's don't think of anything but having fun today."

They passed through a prairie-dog town, little mounds that were scattered over the meadow like a design of close polka dots. Before a few of their holes the prairie dogs sunned themselves on their haunches, turning their sharp-pointed, inquisitive faces toward the car.

"First cousins to Tip, aren't they?" Doc said. "I like the little things, but we shouldn't have come this way. If we fall into a hole we'll surely break a spring."

But they came out safely on the ridge which stretched like a finger from the buttes that dominated the prairie.

"Are we going by the Indian village?" Pat asked.

It was just ahead; in a few minutes they reached it—circles of stones that had once weighted down the edges of the wig-wams, a large circle which had been used for the chief's tepee and smaller ones grouped around it. They had lain undisturbed since the last time the Sioux had camped here. Before them the prairie spread like a rippling golden satin quilt, tufted with darker puffs of buffalo bushes.

"No one could sneak up on them here," Doc said. "They were out of the way of the buffalo herds too, the herds stayed in the valleys. When the tribe wanted a steak all they needed to do was to sharpen an arrow."

"Do you suppose Sitting Bull ever camped here?"

"I don't imagine so. By the time he came along the Indians were pretty well shut up on their reservation over west toward the Missouri River, the Badlands and the Black Hills."

"What made General Custer go into it and fight them?" Pat asked. "Sketch always said Sitting Bull got a raw deal."

Doc twisted the wheel to avoid a badger hole. They bounced into it and out again; his foot came down so heavily on the gas that the car shot forward like a frightened rabbit.

"What, honey? Why did General Custer take that expedition into the Black Hills? Gold. That was what stirred up the rum-pus. When word got around that 'there was gold in them thar hills,' the rush was on. The government did try to keep the whites out, but when people found gold lying loose around Deadwood and Lead and saw that all they had to do was to stick a sieve in the streams and drain it out, it would have taken more than the U. S. Army to stop them. And besides, the army didn't want to stop them; it was all for fighting the Indians. Naturally, Sitting Bull's people rose to protect their reservation, it was all they had left. That wasn't seventy-five years ago. There are still old-timers around who knew Custer and Sitting Bull. That Indian was a real medicine man, the last great leader of his people."

Pat's eyes glowed. She had forgotten her own troubles, she was imagining herself an Indian girl riding a piebald pony bareback along the edge of the draws, keeping in the shadow of the pines or following the thickets, hiding from the army.

Now they had reached the buttes. They were on a high plateau broken by wide draws as steep as little ravines. The path wound through patches of stunted pines.

"Let's stop and look over the edge," Pat suggested. She and Doc climbed out and walked to the edge of the plateau where perpendicular cliffs dropped to the prairie. Hanging on a pine branch, she leaned over.

"These buttes look as though they'd crumble if you put your weight on them."

"Probably would, too. They're just soft stuff like shale, made by water eating them away," Doc said.

The cliff that jutted out like a buttress from the walls on which they were standing dropped sheer and bare but softly colored, ridged with pastel layers of pink, pale green, yellow, golden brown.

"Like a party cake," Pat said.

"Yes, and a long time baking. Each layer took hundreds, maybe thousands of years to make. Getting hungry?"

Pat nodded.

"Over there's a nice flat rock. We can sit on the edge of the cliff and see a large slice of North Dakota."

As they lifted the basket from the car they flushed a buck and five does on the other side of a draw. The buck stood motionless for several minutes, looking at them with his head high, then turned and bounded over the hill, followed by the does. Pat was afraid Doc would try to get him, but he made no motion toward his gun.

"Fine fellow, wasn't he? What an air they have. They all look like princes or ambassadors. I never saw one lose his dignity."

Pat spread paper napkins on the rock and weighted them down with twigs. Doc took out the thermos. He poured coffee into two paper cups while Pat spread the cake and sandwiches on the rock. She looked down. The castellated rainbow walls made a wide semicircle and below them the prairie lay spread out like a map. A ranch house and its outbuildings were immediately beneath them, white-faced Herefords grazed in the fields, a flock of sheep made gray patches around a water hole. Farther away a red truck moved along a pale line that must have been a highway. Pat bit into a sandwich and drank the coffee. The cup felt warm and pleasant in her hand. The anxieties of the last few weeks seemed insignificant and very far away.

Doc took his pipe out of his pocket and lit it; the smoke curled up lazily. It was good to see the shadows gone from Pat's face. What she needed was playmates with whom she could work off her surplus energy. The next best thing was the colt, if Margaret could only see it that way. He fell to wondering what sort of child Margaret had been. Was she always content to reproduce her mother's life in make-believe, with her acorn cups and saucers and her corncob dolls? Yes, he supposed, she had been. Probably she never wanted to play explorer and investigate what lay over the edge of the prairie.

When Pat had eaten the last bite of cake and brushed the crumbs over the cliff, she jumped up and began to explore the pine woods. Across a draw she spied some ripe buffalo berries and ran to pick them for Margaret. Doc watched her contentedly. How mercurial she was, eager and quick, bubbling with life. Sketch all over. He had squeezed the most out of every minute. But he was tough, he had known how to protect his capacity for enjoyment. Pat was too wide-eyed, too generous with herself. He wished he were wise enough to protect her.

In a few minutes she came back with two cupsful of scarlet berries, balancing one on top of the other and carrying in her other hand what looked like a heavy stick.

"Look at this. Somebody's lost a rifle. It has been here a long time and must be very old."

Doc took the rifle and brushed off the dirt.

"Do you know what this is?" His voice was sharp with excitement. "It's an old army rifle, the kind they used before the Spanish-American War. Pat, I think you have found one of the rifles that belonged to Custer's men. You know there was a battle right here in the Slim Buttes. Another detachment of the army met a party of Indians coming back from the massacre and they were loaded down with loot from Custer's troops."

He polished it with his handkerchief.

"It's in pretty good condition too. If it were oiled up I shouldn't be surprised if it would shoot."

Pat's eyes danced.

"Shall we take it home? It's magic. Don't laugh, but I think Old Sitting Bull dropped it here on purpose. He must have known I'd want a present for mother."

Chapter 7

The Water Hole

Margaret was delighted with the rifle and put it on the kitchen wall over the cupboard that held the wedding ring china. She told Pat stories about the massacre on the Little Big Horn that she had heard when she was a child. The horse, the only creature that escaped alive, intrigued Pat. She wondered what had become of him; had some trapper or rancher found him and kept him to a good old age? Margaret wasn't sure but she half remembered that he was recovered by the army and buried somewhere in a military cemetery.

"Ask Ty," she said. "He knows a lot about our history."

But the next time Pat went to the Chisholms she had other things on her mind. There was no one around except Ma.

"Come on in, Patty, and rest your feet. I expected to see you riding on your charger. Doc tells me you've broken him to the saddle."

Pat told Ma how Harmony had become accustomed to the saddle, even with the bridle tied to it and the stirrups dangling. Doc had roped a sack of oats to the saddle and the colt behaved very well but now she was at a standstill.

"I know I could ride him but Mommy won't let me mount him by myself, so I have to wait until Doc comes again."

"That's the way it is, honey. We women are always waiting for a man to come along and help us with whatever we want to do. Would you like to ride now? Jake's shifting the horses to the far pasture and if you want to saddle Old Indian, who's in the corral, you can catch up with him. Jake will be right glad of your help and, who knows, if you talk pretty he may offer to do your snubbing for you."

Pat kissed Ma on her plump cheek. There was something so comforting about Ma that you kept wanting to tell her how much you loved her. Old Indian wanted to stay in the shade of the barn, but Pat threw the saddle on him and walked him slowly across the pasture in the direction of the buttes. Presently she saw Jake with the horses and waved to him.

"Hi, partner," he called when she was near enough to hear. They rode along slowly together, not pushing the horses. It was a drowsy day, not a cloud to break the faded blue of the sky that rested languidly on the edge of the prairie. Even before she mentioned Harmony, Jake asked how she was getting along with him and offered to ride over the next day and snub the colt to his saddle while she mounted him. Pat was so happy that she wanted to gallop to the edge of the prairie, but Old Indian wasn't a horse who wanted to have a fling. He took his time and kept his eyes on the ground, looking for prairie-dog holes.

When they had turned the horses into the far pasture and hooked the gate, Jake rode to a draw that made a smudge on the tawny prairie and dismounted in the shade of a group of stunted willows.

"Let's sit down and cool off a minute. You can let Old Indian go. He'll stand."

He and Pat sat on the edge of the draw with their feet sticking over the bank. Jake plucked a piece of buffalo grass and chewed it lazily.

"What would you think if I bought myself a plane?" he asked suddenly.

"What do you mean? An airplane? The kind you flew in the war? That held sixty people? Where would you find that many around here to go riding in it?"

"You're talking about a transport plane. I didn't mean that kind. Mr. Lennox has bought a Navion, a very plush little four-passenger job. It takes him two days to drive from Kansas City and he can fly in less than five hours. He's coming in this after-noon. I've saved my severance pay for over a year. Pretty good of me, don't you think? I couldn't buy a Navion and I really don't need one, but I could get a little two-seater, a Piper Cub; there are already a lot of them in this country, and they don't cost so awfully much. Lily would love one. When something goes wrong with the truck or the power pump and I have to get a new part I could go to Rapid City in an hour. We could hop into it and go to a dance once in a while, or a movie. You can even put runners on them in the winter and take off in the snow."

Pat stared at him with open mouth.

"A plane right here at Ma's! I think it would be wonderful. What would you name it? They had such funny names during the war. And you wouldn't paint a dragon's face on it?"

"Nope," Jake said, scratching two wings in the dust, "just a nice little red one, maybe with Lily's initials on the door. When I got out of the navy I thought I never wanted to put my hand on another joy stick. But that was two years ago and it seems a thousand. Now I want to fly again. But don't say anything to Ma about it yet. You'd think I wasn't out of knee pants, the way she worries about me."

Jake stood up and gave Pat a hand, out of the ditch. They mounted their horses and pointed back toward the house. She had intended to tell him about Harmony, but the plane was something different to think about. She tried to imagine what it would feel like to be high up in the sky with everything below looking flat on top.

The house seemed deserted. She and Jake turned their horses into the corral and went into the kitchen. Ma was sitting over a cup of coffee by herself.

"What time do you expect Mr. Lennox?" Ma asked.

"Anytime now." Jake looked out the window toward the south. "He was a transport pilot in the war, delivering them over the hump to China, so he ought to get along all right."

"I wonder if it's cool up there." Ma fanned herself with a palm leaf fan. "Even if it is, I guess I'll have to be content with the legs the Lord gave me and not go coveting wings."

Jake stood up and stuck his head out the door, listening.

"Look, Pat, here he comes." He pointed to a tiny dark speck no bigger than a pea. In a few minutes the plane was circling over the ranch like an enormous blue dragonfly. It slid down on the prairie in front of the barn and taxied to a stop. Jake already was examining the two gaily-painted wings and the glass-enclosed cockpit. The seats were upholstered in a pale gray. It looked like an elegant miniature sedan with wings.

"How is she?" he asked.

Mr. Lennox climbed out and stood back, admiring it.

"Sweetest little engine you ever heard. I had a tail wind most of the way and made it in about three and one-half hours. Hello, cowboy, what do you think of her?"

"May I sit inside, just for fun?"

"Tell you what, I'm going up to speak to Ma. She's my best girl and I'll ask her if she'd like to go for a ride. If she won't, and seeing that she thinks we are horning in on the prerequisites of the angels, I don't think she will, I'll take you. How's that?"

Pat grinned.

Carrying his bag, Mr. Lennox went to the kitchen door. While he was gone Jake climbed in and looked at the controls.

In a few minutes Mr. Lennox came back laughing and shaking his head.

"I guess you get the ride, my girl. I won't be long, Jake, for I know you're itching to get your hands on it."

He helped Pat in and showed her how to fasten the belt. Jake gave the propeller a whirl and they taxied a piece to prepare for a take-off. Before Pat realized that she had left the ground, they were air-borne and circling over the ranch house. Mr. Lennox wasn't taking her straight home, that would have taken but a couple of minutes; he was making a wide circle over Strool with its post office and store and a half-dozen cars parked in the street, over the Lancaster ranch and along the edge of the buttes where an eagle rose from a ledge and took a look at them. Below, the cattle were stationary dots no larger than a shirt button, and on a rise a herd of antelope showed their tails and white rumps like so many tiny powder puffs.

"It makes you feel just like God going out after breakfast to see how he likes his world." Pat sighed with delight.

"I wonder if He misses the buffaloes." Mr. Lennox was looking down on the land that from the air seemed flat and bald, traversed by cracks and pushed up in enormous greenish-brown bubbles. "Wouldn't you have liked to see the buffaloes? From up here they would have made the ground look as if some giant had overturned his pepper pot. My father remembers when Eastern sportsmen came out to hunt them and found so many that they shot wantonly into the herds and let them die, never even bothering to skin the carcasses."

"Jake says there is a creek bed farther west in the buttes where you can see the bones of buffaloes that were killed in a stampede."

"We'll go look for them sometime. That's your house, isn't it?"

When they straightened out for a landing, Margaret came running from the kitchen, shading her eyes. The blue-winged creature rolled up not far from her feet. Mr. Lennox jumped down and gave Pat a hand. Margaret walked over and touched the nearest wing.

"I never thought I'd see a plane here at my own door. It's as saucy as a blue jay. What are you going to do with it?"

"Practically everything except herd cattle. Planes are what this country needs. When you can get to Rapid City in an hour and Pierre in less than two, you won't mind being sixty miles from a railroad."

"I don't mind now," Margaret said. "I love this country just as it is." She led the way into the kitchen.

"You and the buffaloes." He smiled at her and his smile included Pat.

"I'll make some tea." To Pat's astonishment Margaret took down the wedding ring teapot. Pat sat on the edge of her chair and fidgeted. She was glad Margaret had taken off the faded jeans in which she cleaned the chicken house and was wearing a fresh dress, but she wasn't interested in polite tea talk.

"Doc says you have a jumper that has won a lot of prizes and that you're going to bring her out here for the winter."

"That I am and next year I'll train two or three of Ty's best colts. I've always wanted to breed them myself as well as show them. That's what I'm planning to do with the ranch."

"Harmony's a good jumper too. I could show him to you if you'd like. He's down by the creek. It won't take a minute to get him."

"Good." Mr. Lennox held out his cup for more tea. Pat had a feeling that he was far more eager to talk with Margaret than he was to see Harmony, but she wanted to show him the colt. She ran to the barn for the halter, but it wasn't on the nail. She must have forgotten to take it off of Harmony when she turned him out. She went down toward the creek. Harmony wasn't in sight; probably he was on the other side hidden by the thicket of willows and buffalo berries. As she neared the creek, she called; usually Harmony stuck his head through the bushes, but this time there was no sign of him. By the water hole, a spot in the creek which had been dammed to hold some of the water that flooded it in the spring, but by midsummer left it as dry as a picked turkey bone, she heard a yelping, high and urgent.

"Tip," she shouted, and plunged through the thicket. In the water hole that had been churned to mud by his flailing hoofs, Harmony stood up to his belly in mire. One end of his halter had come loose and his front foot was tangled in the rope; every step he took had led him farther into the hole. His back and mane were plastered and there were patches of mud on his face. When he saw Pat he gave a mighty heave, but his legs held fast.

"Don't struggle," she called. "I'll get you out." He laid back his ears and turned to her, eyes full of terror. Tip danced around the edge of the muck, howling at the top of his voice. Pat saw that she must first cut the halter. She knew what to do next as she had seen the Lancasters pull cows out of water holes, but she needed help: a few planks to put in front of the colt to hold solid when he got his forefeet free and needed leverage to drag out his back legs, a large rope to put around his neck and a car to pull. Maybe Mr. Lennox would help. She didn't want to leave Harmony in the mud until Jake could get there. She ran, panting, back across the meadow, but as she came in sight of the house she saw Margaret and Mr. Lennox walk out to the plane. He twirled the propeller, got in and taxied for a start. A moment later the plane rose in a graceful sweep and came toward her. She semaphored frantically; he leaned out to smile at her and wave good-by.

"He couldn't wait to see Harmony this time," Margaret explained, "but he wants to come again." Pat didn't listen.

"Harmony's stuck in the water hole. I've got to get Jake or somebody, quick."

Margaret brushed the hair from Pat's flushed cheeks.

"Don't get excited. Maybe we can do it. I've often helped your grandfather get cows out of the mud." She pulled her dress over her head, hung it in the closet and stepped into a pair of jeans. Pat waited, fiddling at the catch of the door. How could her mother take so long! When she had slipped on her work blouse, Margaret took Pat's hand and held her back.

"Don't get all worn out before we start."

Pat was carrying the sharpest kitchen knife. She tossed the snubbing rope into the car and helped Margaret stick several old planks crosswise through the open back doors. Margaret stepped on the starter. The Ford gave an unwilling grunt and began to roll across the prairie. Luckily, beyond the water hole the creek bed widened. Finding a clearing in the bushes where the bank had caved in, she drove the Ford through it and hit the creek with such a thud that the boards jounced out. Turning back up the gravel bed, she stopped just beyond the dam. Harmony was twisting and straining, but he had made no progress. Tip ran to them and leaped upon Pat, yelping and clawing at her hands.

Margaret looked at the horse a minute, speculating. Pat had jumped out and waded into the mud. She sawed on the rope with the knife. It was not a heavy one and the strands cut easily. With his foot released Harmony reared his head and tried to pull out, but he was stuck fast. Pat stroked his neck to quiet him.

"I think we can get a couple of these planks under his belly," Margaret called. "I'll push and you get a stick to dig at the mud on the other side." She slid one of the boards toward Harmony and pushed. His belly was barely resting on the mud. Pat laid a board on the other side of Harmony, to kneel on while she cleared away the mud that was plowed up by the end of the board. Margaret pushed through another board.

"That ought to help. Now let's put the others in front of him." Pat stroked Harmony's nose and felt him nuzzling her

Pat laid a board on the other side.

arm. She adjusted the rope around his neck. This was going to
hurt. She tied the free end to the bumper of the car, Margaret
got in and seeing the anxiety in Pat's face she leaned out and
blew her a kiss.

"Don't worry. I'll barely start it, just enough to give him a
lift."

The starter buzzed, Margaret let in the clutch very slowly,
the rope slipped up Harmony's neck to his head bones and stuck
behind his ears. It tautened, he gasped and his tongue hung out.
With a sucking noise the mud began to give him up.

"Stop, stop!" shouted Pat. "He's choking." Margaret threw
out the clutch. The rope slacked a little, Harmony took a gasping breath and forced his right foot from the mire. Bracing it
on the plank, he pulled out the other but his haunches wouldn't
come. Pat untied the rope.

"We can't pull him any more by the neck, we've burned it
already."

"Put the rope behind his front legs and under his shoulders,"
Margaret directed. "I think one little pull will do it." With the
noose adjusted around his barrel, Margaret cautiously let in the
clutch. This time Harmony was able to help and with a great
heave he loosened his back legs and planted them on the board
that Margaret had pushed under his belly. Tip, who had stood
by, without making a sound, as though he understood that he
mustn't get in the way, leaped up and down in a frenzy and
tried to lick Harmony's nose.

On firm ground the colt breathed hoarsely, scarcely able to
stand on his trembling legs.

"He's done in. I'll go along with the car. You'd better let him
take his time."

The Ford jolted off across the meadow. The mud already
was beginning to harden on Harmony's coat; Pat knocked some
of it loose.

"You look almost as miserable as you did when Jake found

you, but you've got more strength. You can make it to the barn." She started him along, leading him by the broken halter. Harmony stayed close to her, taking a few steps, resting, taking a few more as his legs got stronger. She stroked his neck, his back and thighs. Tip ran at the colt's heels, sometimes darting out in front and barking at him, encouraging him. So they progressed across the hay meadow to the barn, the girl, the horse and the dog, sustaining each other.

When Harmony was safely in his stall, Pat flew to get water and a sponge. It was suppertime before she finished cleaning off the mud. When Margaret called, Pat gave Harmony a final rub and put on his blanket. Then she gave him his bran mash that Margaret had heated for her and kissed the white star on his face.

"You'll be all right now, boy. Come on, Tip, do you want your supper?" But the little dog was curled up in the fresh straw and wouldn't move. "All right, you stay here and nurse him. I'll bring your supper after a while."

Pat ran into the kitchen and scrubbed her hands in the wash basin under the window, sniffing the chicken in the frying pan.

"Mummy," she cried, throwing her arms around Margaret's neck and knocking the fork out of her hand, "you're just about the nicest Mummy in the world."

Margaret held her daughter tight for a moment, stroking her cheek. Then she pushed her away gently and reached for the fork.

"Well, after all, you're the only Pat I have."

Chapter 8

Feeling His Oats

Pat was tired. She didn't wait to brush her hair, but fell into bed and lay there, not thinking, not feeling, just enjoying the cool sheets and the peaceful, trancelike state of relaxed muscles. Presently she drifted into light, confused dreams in which she was galloping in a pasture that was all mixed up with the sky. She and Harmony were taking off in the open blue skies and skimming over banks of clouds, around and around, sometimes between little hills of them and again over them, smooth as satin, never breaking pace.

Hours or minutes later she opened her eyes and lay rigid in her bed, cold with fright. Her eyes strained but saw nothing. Outside the window the night was black, the moon had gone down and there was not enough light to cast a shadow. Her ears strained but there was no sound except the vague whispering of the wind in the buffalo grass or, yes, there was a sound, very faint and distant. Tip was barking. As the sound became more urgent the blood began to pound in Pat's temples. Breaking the paralysis that held her, she jumped out of bed and darted to the window. She leaned out but everything was still. Tip wasn't barking and yet she kept on hearing him somewhere inside her head.

"Harmony! It's Harmony. Something's the matter."

Slipping into her jeans she tiptoed into the kitchen. Margaret's door always stood ajar, but she was sleeping; Pat could hear her regular breathing. Feeling her way to the stove, Pat found the matches; at the back door, she ran her hand up the side of the frame for the nail that held the lantern. Stepping outside and closing the door behind her, she lit the lantern. The blackness pressed in around her as she ran across to the corral, unbolted the gate and crossed to the stable. Tip ran out to meet her. He was barking now, but it was just a welcome yap.

Pat held up the lantern and looked into the box stall. Harmony opened his eyes and blinked, then flicked his ears at her and went back to sleep. He was breathing naturally. She felt his nose and ran her hand over his neck. His skin was cool— no fever. Nothing was the matter, she was just being silly, frightened by a dream, but the impression of it was so vivid that she couldn't shake it off. Maybe it was meant to warn her that something was going to happen to Harmony. She couldn't bring herself to leave him; she spread a pile of sacking on the floor, turned down the lantern to a tiny flame and hung it on a nail in the doorway, lay down on the sacks and pulled one of them over her. If Harmony should get sick during the night she would be with him.

She wasn't afraid, none of the farmyard noises disturbed her; but she had never slept anywhere except in her own bed in the familiar pink room, and the strangeness of the shadows, the dangling fringe of grass from the hayloft, the gleam of the lantern light on the tines of the forks standing against the wall, filled her with a vague uneasiness. Tip had snuggled against her. She thrust out her hand and touched his paw. He moved closer and licked her ear.

When she awakened it was broad daylight. Tip was chasing the chickens in the yard and Harmony was sticking his head over the stall door, looking for his breakfast.

"Pat! Pat!" Margaret was calling her. She ran to the kitchen, brushing off the dust and hay.

"What a sight you are. Hurry and wash your face."

Her mother didn't know she had spent the night in the barn. Pat felt relieved as she scrubbed her hands. She would fill the lantern and slip it back on the nail, no one need know of her foolishness.

After breakfast she fed Harmony and turned him into the corral, then cleaned the bridle and saddle to be ready for Jake. He came along in midmorning, riding one of his cow ponies with a western saddle. Pat was in the soddy; she did not run out to meet him, not until he had talked with Margaret. The two of them stood laughing in the kitchen doorway. Presently Jake came across to the soddy.

"Pretty nice tackroom you have. I'll bet this is one of the last soddies left around here. Ours is nothing but a mound of dirt." He picked up the saddle and handed her the bridle.

Harmony was feeling good. The morning was crisp and fresh and he had suffered nothing from his mud bath but weariness and a scraped neck. He didn't like the corral; he wanted to get out to the pasture, but Pat had closed the gate with a wire.

"That can't be little starface!" Jake exclaimed. "That's a real horse, a grand creature. There's nothing the matter with his bones."

"And you should see him jump. Doc says he has good form," Pat said proudly.

Jake told Pat to put on the bridle since Harmony was accustomed to her. She tried to catch his halter, but first he wanted to play and he wouldn't stand until she had chased him across the corral a couple of times. While Jake held the bridle she slipped the saddle over the colt's back. He kicked and bucked a few times just to show his spirit.

"The girth isn't tight enough. The devil is blowing himself up and holding his breath. We'll take him out into the pasture

and walk him around a bit. That's an old trick, fellow. You can't
get away with it."

Pat led Harmony into the pasture and a few minutes later
the colt let Jake tighten the strap. Jake went back to the house
for his cow pony and rode him close to Harmony. Unwinding
a rope from the pommel, he told Pat to slip the noose over Harmony's head and run the rope through the bridle ring. The colt
reared, but before he had time to run out with the rope, Jake
had wound it around the pommel and had him snubbed to
within a couple of feet, with his nose almost buried in the cow
pony's side.

Harmony kicked and twisted but he couldn't pull loose. Remembering other snubbing ropes, he quieted down. There
wasn't much a horse could do when he couldn't get his head.
Pat talked to him and when he was quiet, stroked his face.

"Now get up as lightly as you can," Jake instructed.

Pat put her foot in the stirrup and swung on so gently that
Harmony only side-stepped a little. For a minute he stood as
though he were thinking what to do, then jerked his head and
pulled back with all his strength, but Jake and the cow pony
held firm; the colt couldn't widen the distance from the pony's
side.

Pat sat lightly, clinging with her knees, her blood pounding.
Automatically Harmony tried all of his tricks again, but not
with conviction; he knew he couldn't shake her off with his
head held tight. When he was tired of pulling the rope that hurt
his burned neck, Jake let it out a little. Within an hour he and
Pat were racing across the pasture with Harmony at the end
of the rope.

"Slip it now," he called, "and get a good grip on your lines.
I'm going to let you go it alone, but I'll be right with you."

Pat slipped the noose. Harmony, feeling his freedom, set out
across the prairie, his neck extended, his hoofs chopping the
sod. Jake rode beside her. She could see him out of the tail of

her eye, but she didn't look around; she had all she could do to keep her seat. It was a glorious ride with the wind cutting her face. Harmony was not fighting her, he was one with her, feeling the same intoxication. When his own horse began to tire, Jake reached for Pat's bridle and turned Harmony toward home. At the corral Jake told Pat that now while the colt was tired she should mount and dismount a few times. She did, with Jake holding the bridle; even when he gave her the reins, Harmony only quivered as though he were brushing a fly off his back.

"I believe you can manage him now," Jake said, "but I'd cut down the oats for a little while and let him do his jumps first to get some of the liveliness out of him. You've done a marvelous job." He ran his hands over Harmony's thighs.

"He's certainly filled out. If I were you I wouldn't ride him over the jumps until he becomes accustomed to you in the saddle. Jumping is quite different from riding—your seat, what you do with the reins, everything. I'm not a hunter. Get Doc to start you right."

Jake rode back to the house to say good-by to Margaret. She had been standing in the doorway with her hands clenched under her apron.

"You see, it's all right. That colt hasn't a mean bone in his body. Pat will get a lot of fun out of him."

Margaret tried to smile but her lips were stiff.

"Yes, if I can stand it."

"Mummy, may I ride Harmony to school?" For a week Pat had been riding him every day and most of the day until Margaret's nerves were ragged.

"No," she said, "I want you to go in the Ford with me and help me take things."

On the first Monday of October, Pat was up at daylight to clean and feed Harmony before breakfast. As Margaret was expected to start the furnace in the schoolhouse and warm the room before the children came, she and Pat left home at seven-thirty. It was only about two miles to the schoolhouse, but she allowed herself a half hour in case the Ford wouldn't start.

Pat had reconciled herself to leaving Harmony. She could ride him in the afternoons and on Saturdays and Sundays. She felt the tenseness of Margaret's nerves and wished she could help. School wouldn't be hard if Margaret knew how to get along with children, but they could be demons if they wanted to. Pat remembered how they had plagued a substitute who had tried to hold school once when Miss Nancy was sick. Margaret never had known any child except Pat. Would she ignore Bob Lancaster's stubborn streaks and pay no attention to Nancy Yates who thought she was going to die every time she scratched her finger? Pat wished she could say these things to Margaret, but knew it wouldn't do. Margaret was fighting her doubts alone and it would have upset her to know how much Pat understood.

It was a raw morning; the wind pushed the Ford about and tumbleweed danced ahead of them into the fences. Pat opened the barbed wire gate that kept the cattle out of the schoolyard. The square white building with its two little outhouses might have been cut out and pasted on a piece of sand-colored cardboard.

Margaret unlocked the door and went to the basement to start the fire. Pat drew a bucket of water and put it beside the wash basin on the shelf in the little entrance hall. Out of her schoolbag she pulled a towel and a brand new cake of soap. The blackboards were clean, but some of the last year's drawings of Easter tulips remained stuck on the windowpanes. By the time Margaret came up from the basement and washed her hands, the windows were clean, the room swept and dusted and the eight desks arranged before the teacher's large one, the smallest desks in front.

Margaret set up her books on the desk.

"Thank you. I never could have done it all."

"It won't be so hard tomorrow morning." Pat looked out of the window, the children were coming, Bob and Jane Lancaster were tying their ponies in the shed. The Yates children arrived in a truck. Their father dropped them at the gate and called to Margaret that he would bring some groceries from town. Before it was time to ring the bell, Mrs. Johnson drove up with Johnny and Ruby, and little Eric Schwartz dressed in a Hopalong Cassidy suit and cowboy boots. Margaret helped them take off their wraps and herded them to their seats. The clock on her desk said nine, she tapped her pencil, they rose to repeat the allegiance to the flag, little Ruby and Eric watching with open mouths. Then they sat down and waited. This was the anxious moment; could Margaret get them organized before they began to think of mischief or would they sense her inexperience? Pat sat watching Bob the troublemaker who was so full of vitality that he hated the restraints of school. She dared not offer to help for she could not afford to be branded as Mother's pet; but she need not have worried. Margaret lost her nervousness when she was actually confronted with the children. She set the lessons briskly and even had young Eric engaged in copying a big *A* on his slate before he had time to wiggle.

It was going to be all right. Pat settled back at her desk next to the window and opened her history book. This year she and Bob were studying the history of South Dakota. Soon she was absorbed in the first chapter. She had not known that South Dakota was an old, old land and that its layers of soft rock were one of the richest fossil areas of the world. West of the Missouri River, the book said, scientists had found the bones of strange sea creatures who lived thousands of years ago when the country was an enormous lake called the Cambrian Sea. And east of the river where the great ice sheet had stretched, they had found in the petrified forests skeletons of prehistoric animals,

giant creatures as long as a barn and as high as a house, dino-
saurs and giant pigs, as well as midget deer, camels two feet
high and three-toed horses no larger than a sheep.

While she heard the sixth grade reading lesson, Margaret
sent Pat and Bob to the blackboard to draw the prehistoric animals to scale, compared with their descendants. Pinned to the
board were pictures of the creatures; but for the modern animals they had to depend on their own memories. Bob wanted to
choose the saber-toothed tiger but he couldn't remember the
shape of the tiger he had seen in a circus so he settled on the
three-toed horse. Pat took the midget camel although she wasn't
sure how high the camel of today stood. The llama was a de-
scendant too, but she couldn't even remember a picture of the
creature.

Bob was briskly sketching his horse's extra toe.

"Did you know I rode in the rodeo last week at Bison?" he
whispered. Pat's eyes glowed.

"Your father let you?"

"Sure. I won fifty dollars. Dad wouldn't let me have it, he
put it in the bank for me. That bronc landed me on my shoulder. See." He rolled up his sleeve and showed her the edge of
a bruise as though it were a *Croix de guerre.*

"And I can pick up a handkerchief. I've been practicing it all
summer."

"Well, I bet next summer I can beat you. I'm going to practice, too, now that I can ride Harmony."

"Look, silly, what you've done. That runt didn't have a
hump."

Pat hastily erased the hump from the prehistoric camel.

"Harmony's going to be a jumper. He can already clear three
feet."

Bob was so interested that he carelessly gave his horse another toe.

"Suppose I ride over Saturday. Maybe we can practice some."

Pat nodded. Margaret rang the bell for recess. Pat and Bob went to the shed to see how his mare, Cindy, was getting along.

"Want to see how I can pick up a handkerchief?"

They took Cindy out of the gate onto the prairie. He asked Pat to take off her kerchief and throw it on the ground, then rode Cindy toward it at a lively canter. As he approached the kerchief he slid sidewise out of the saddle, holding on with one hand and, leaning with his head almost touching the ground, snatched her kerchief from the grass. She watched with round, envious eyes. He recovered his seat and rode up to her, holding out the kerchief.

"I can't do it at a gallop yet, but it just takes practice."

Margaret had come to the door to ring the bell. She saw the children lined along the fence watching the show. As they came in she took Bob aside.

"I'll be glad if you won't ride your horse during school hours," she said. "When you give them a circus the children won't want to think about their lessons." Bob flushed. Pat watched anxiously, hoping he wouldn't answer back. "I hear you won a prize in the Bison rodeo," Margaret continued. "I wish I had seen you."

Pat could have hugged her.

By the time school was out the day was bright, the wind had died and it was perfect riding weather. She could hardly wait to get back to Harmony, but she couldn't leave Margaret. Mrs. Johnson was late coming for Johnny and Ruby and as she left the yard Mr. Yates' truck came up the road. He lifted out a large box of groceries, canned soup, beans, crackers, orange juice.

"Here you are. We probably won't have a blizzard yet a while, but we might as well get in our stock." He put it on Margaret's desk and smiled at his children. "Hope you didn't have to wear out a switch on 'em today."

Margaret walked to the door with him and waved them off.

Mr. Yates was a member of the school board and she hoped he would carry home a good impression. She began to unload the box.

"I guess we'd best put these in the cellar."

"Mummy, if you'll leave them till morning, I'll take them all down before school. I promise. It's such a lovely afternoon."

Margaret hesitated, she looked at the cans and then at Pat's anxious eyes.

"All right, honey. Get our books. I'll lock the door."

Pat threw her arms around Margaret and this time she got an answering hug.

Chapter 9

The Wolf

Autumn stretched out in an infinity of golden days, and on every one of them Pat worked with Harmony. Doc stopped by often and he was a strict riding master. When he was convinced that Harmony recognized Pat and the saddle as natural appendages he drilled her in jumping, showed her how to gauge the moment to take off, how to count one and two and on three give the command by a pressure of the knees, at the same moment rising in the saddle, leaning forward, practically over the horse's neck and taking the jump with him.

"It's right to hold a tight rein on the approach," he said, "but when you lean forward to take off, you want literally to throw the reins away. Harmony can't jump unless he has his head. Then tighten up when he comes down, just enough to keep him from running out on either side. Now try it again. Don't be afraid to lean forward all the way. Take your weight off his back. You're jumping with him."

And Pat tried until Doc was almost satisfied. It seemed unnatural for her to throw the reins away; not for weeks did she manage a take off that really pleased Doc.

"When I'm not here," he warned her, "don't let up and don't get careless and uncritical."

[82]

He took Harmony over the jumps himself and told her to watch his hands and his seat.

"I know it's hard for you to do it alone, it's so much easier when you see it done, but we'll learn one way or another, won't we, Patty?"

So Pat worked faithfully and after the lessons she and Harmony rode over the prairie. Sometimes when they were loafing in the meadow with Harmony occasionally nibbling at a clump of grass it was as though these moments were the only ones that ever had existed or ever would. The child she had been was somebody else, a little girl whom she had barely known, and next year or the following one she could not imagine. The grown-up Pat, even the one she dreamed about, the fine Pat in the riding boots and derby, was a stranger too. This was real, Harmony under her, straining against the bridle, the scent of sagebrush and the crackle of dry sunflower stalks, the feel of her own muscles responding to his. Harmony was hers; they belonged to each other. It would be this way always. She would keep it this way; nothing could change it.

Yet perceptibly the days shortened, the dark closed in earlier and earlier, dropping like a soft black blanket over the pasture. One moment you saw the sky behind the creek bordered with flame and gold and the next the whole world was blotted out. After school there was scarcely enough time to do the chores before Margaret switched on the lights and stirred up the fire for supper. Then she and Pat sat next to the comfort of the kitchen stove and did their lessons.

The afternoons were gone but the week-ends were Pat's own. On Saturdays Margaret drove to Strool for the week's groceries and Pat spent the day with Harmony. Sometimes Bob Lancaster came over, riding Cindy and they practiced in the meadow behind the barn. Pat had arranged three jumps, a two-and-one-half-foot rail, bales of hay two high, and a three-foot rail, spaced, according to Doc's directions, twenty-six feet apart so that Harmony could collect himself between them.

Cindy didn't like to jump and Bob didn't urge her. She came up to the rail cautiously, pawed at it with a dainty foot, knocked it off the boxes and jumped aside. She would dash at great speed and wheel on a dime; she was quick on the getaway and had a stop that Bob was especially proud of; she rounded up cattle without even the pressure of a finger on her reins; she could canter through the figures of a quadrille at the rodeo and she liked such tricks as picking up handkerchiefs, but as for jumping—she watched Harmony with bored disdain as if she wondered why in the world he was doing such silly things. Bob patted her and did not ask her to try again. He was teaching her to kneel; soon, he bragged, she would do as well as Roy Rogers' palomino.

Margaret, at her work, watched them from the kitchen window. For some reason that she did not analyze she was not distressed to leave Bob and Pat playing in the meadow, not even when she saw Pat jumping bareback. She was not particularly afraid of mishaps although she had been pretending so to herself; she trusted Pat's judgment and her skill as a rider. When Bob and Cindy were with him Harmony seemed reduced in importance, he was just an ordinary colt, no longer a symbol of that alien world which had drawn Sketch and was now attracting Pat away from her. When Doc was training Pat her resentment was so strong that she did not trust herself at the window. He and Sketch were in league against her, but Bob was an ally; he belonged to her life, he was as much a part of it as the prairie, the log house and the corral. So she waved to them when she came out to start the Ford and called that there were fresh cookies in the box. Pat could not understand her mother's sudden change of mood but accepted it gladly, thankful to be free of her disapproval.

So on these October Saturdays, she and Bob practiced and

occasionally, when Mr. Lancaster needed them, they rode into the buttes to help him look for cattle. He had driven home the sheep which had been pastured in the buttes all summer and sent Margaret's over to the hay meadow where the grass was good and there was water. It was time now to bring in the stock where they could be fed when the big snows came.

The sheep had been herded into the creek pasture on a school day. Pat saw them there when she came home and wondered if Harmony would look upon them as usurpers. He and Tip were close to them; Harmony grazing placidly and Tip pretending that he was a sheep dog, every so often barking at the fat gray bundles with their little pointed noses and sticklike legs half concealed by a fringe of wool. The sheep paid no attention to Tip and bunched together, nibbling close the grass of which Harmony had eaten only the tops.

"Why, he likes the silly things," Pat decided. "I guess he must be lonely by himself all day." Every afternoon she found him with the sheep. He did not chase them and play with them as he did with Tip, but he grazed close to them, never letting them out of his sight. Sometimes at night he came out of the barn to keep them company. He had long ago learned to open his stall door just as he had the gate of the corral.

In November the first snow fell, thin flakes that clung to the grass like a light sugar frosting. It began in the morning with a flurry of wind from the northwest. By midafternoon the wind had died and the snow had stopped. When the children got out of school they pranced in it like yearlings, tracking it with their boots and smearing each other's faces with wet mittens. The fall was so light that they couldn't gather enough for snowballs. On the way home the Ford slithered over the thin crust. Margaret hung onto the wheel, her eyes bright and her cheeks flushed with the effort to keep it in the track.

"How lovely she is," thought Pat, "when she's excited."

When Pat ran out to clean Harmony's stall she left the collar of her Windbreaker open to feel the crisp air on her skin. Everything glittered, each blade of buffalo grass bent in its sheath of half snow, half ice. Harmony, who was in the pasture, saw her and came charging into the corral, his hoofs kicking up a swirl of white dust. He nuzzled her back impatiently, asking her to play with him.

"All right, starface, we'll let the chickens wait." She zipped up her Windbreaker, threw her leg over his back and caught his mane. He wheeled, ran across the corral and out into the pasture. Straight toward the buttes he raced, the girl clinging to him with her knees, no saddle, no bridle, just she and the horse, like an Indian and his pony breezing across the prairie before the white man had seen it. A pheasant whirred up, startled by Harmony's pounding hoofs, a jackrabbit scuttered before them, the prairie glistened in the pale sun, sparkling like diamond dust.

On Harmony raced toward the buttes. They were coming to the fence; what was she to do? How could she turn him? She yanked on his mane but he paid no more attention to her than if she were a flea. The fence was upon them, she lay forward on his neck as he cleared it, rising in a lovely swift arc.

"Harmony," she gulped, "didn't you know that was barbed wire?"

Fear had gripped her throat but it was elation that almost choked her. Now she knew what Doc had meant by soaring on an eagle's wings.

Harmony ran on, smooth, untiring, the rhythm of his hoof-beats pounding in her ears. Presently he turned of his own volition into the sunset, pale strips of rose and violet reflected on the snow. Now he walked sedately, keeping in the path. Pat relaxed, able to breathe again. When they came to the gate he stopped and waited for her to open it. In a few minutes they were back in the corral. Pat rubbed him down and threw a blanket over him.

"No dinner until you cool off, my lad," she kissed his white star, "but didn't we have fun!"

It was dark by the time Pat had fed the chickens and given Harmony his hay. She was cold now. As she crossed the yard the light through the kitchen window made a fanlike pattern on the snow. Supper was ready.

"You're all lighted up as though you've been swallowing fireflies," Margaret said, filling her plate with stew. Pat sniffed the savory hunks of beef, the carrots, onions and potatoes richly flavored with meat. Even the smell of it gave her a drowsy feeling of repletion. By the time she had eaten two helpings she was so relaxed and drowsy that she thought she would like to sit by the stove forever, napping and baking her tired muscles. Finally she roused herself.

"Mummy, I studied my arithmetic in school. I'm so sleepy, I guess I'll go to bed."

"Good night, sweet. Keep awake long enough to wash your face."

The cold water revived Pat a little; she managed to undress and brush her hair. After she turned out the light she opened the window a crack, not more than a crack for Margaret said the house was full of fresh air; you couldn't expect the kitchen stove to heat the whole outdoors. Pat looked out. It was moonlight, everything black and silver. She could see the fringe of willows and cottonwoods by the creek making a line of delicate interlacing shadows. Nearer the barn the sheep were huddled in a blur of gray dots. They didn't like the snow, she thought, they were bunching up to keep warm. She jumped into her bed and pulled up her grandmother's down comforter, the one covered with a patchwork of her mother's baby dresses, and the next moment she was asleep.

When she awoke the moonlight silvered the window. The moon itself hung in the upper corner of the frame, pale in an indigo sky and opposite it the side of the barn and the edge of

Harmony was a tornado.

its roof made a dark triangle like a picture on the cover of a magazine. The window might have been a print on the wall, everything was motionless, still, no sound except the gentle creaking of the wind generator in the yard. Too still, and chilly. Pat slipped out of bed to close the window. She looked at the undulating white prairie splotched with its own shadows that lay in the hollows like little pools. Near the corral the sheep were huddled. Harmony was with them, his head down and his tail drooping, asleep.

As she stood there shivering but entranced, thinking the prairie was like the beggar maid of the fairy tale who changed into a jeweled princess, she saw a commotion among the sheep. Harmony screamed. She had heard a horse scream once before, one of Sketch's colts that an angry stallion beat to death with his hoofs. The sound pierced to her very marrow and made her spine feel like jelly. Harmony who had been a motionless silhouette the instant before, was a tornado; his figure blurred as he leaped and twisted, flailing with his hoofs, kicking up a mist of snow.

Pat stuck her feet into her shoes, pulled her coat over her pajamas and ran into the kitchen to snatch Sketch's gun from behind the door.

"What is it?" called Margaret.

"Something's after the sheep!"

Margaret sprang out of bed. As she looked behind the kitchen door for the gun she remembered how many times her father had snatched his rifle and stalked out into the dark. Now it was Sketch's rifle that hung on the nail, but he never had been around when she needed a man. As she ran across the yard, crunching the snow, the resentment and yearning that had struggled against each other like weary wrestlers, trampled back and forth over her heart.

When she caught up with Pat she took the gun. The commotion among the sheep had subsided; they were pushing dumbly

against the fence and Harmony stood snorting, furious, his neck
stretched out, looking toward the creek. He was wet and quivering, so shaken that he did not notice Pat when she stroked his
face.

"It must have been a coyote. Harmony wounded him. Look,
the blood." Margaret pointed with the gun to tracks that led
toward the creek. One of them was shallow and blurred as
though something had been dragged along the snow and it was
smeared with dark stains. She looked carefully among the sheep
but could find no dead ones.

"I'm going to drive them into the corral. You'd best put Harmony in his stall and throw a blanket over him." She patted his
wet flank. "I didn't know he could fight like that." Her voice
was warm as though she were proud of him.

"Are we going to leave the coyote? Don't you think we ought
to get him?"

"No, he might be dangerous. He may not be wounded very
badly. We'll tell Jake. He's collecting skins for bounty. Come,
help me with the sheep."

The silly creatures bleated as Pat and Margaret drove them into the corral, nudging against each other with their heads down.
Pat rubbed off Harmony and put his blanket over him. He was
still twitching but he quieted when Tip came in and lay down
in the corner.

"That's all we can do tonight," Margaret said, watching from
the barn door. "Let's go back to bed."

Pat kissed Harmony on the forehead and returned to the
kitchen, stepping in her old tracks in the snow.

Chapter 10

The Blizzard

In the morning as soon as she had put on the coffee, Margaret phoned Jake. He promised to come over in a few minutes; Mr. Lennox was there and they were going hunting in the Navion. As Pat and Margaret turned the Ford into the road on the way to school they saw the blue plane floating serenely through the bright morning. It swooped down over them so low that Pat almost screamed. Mr. Lennox waved and Jake leaned out shaking his rifle. Pat craned her neck to watch them skim over the tops of the cottonwoods along the creek.

When they returned in the late afternoon Mr. Lennox's long convertible was parked behind the kitchen door.

"Company," Margaret said, smoothing her braids.

Mr. Lennox and Jake came out of the kitchen to meet them. How handsome Mr. Lennox was, Pat thought, in his hunting cap and speckled tweed jacket.

"We built up your fire," he said, "and put some coffee on. Jake wanted to raid your cakebox but I restrained him."

The kitchen was so warm that Margaret and Pat took off their coats. Usually they had to wait until the fire burned up. Margaret spread a linen cloth on the table and took down the wedding ring tea set. Jake lifted a bundle of newspapers that he had put behind the door.

"Want to see what was bothering you last night?" He spread out a skin still damp and bloody. "Not a coyote, a wolf. We haven't seen one of these around here for a dozen years. A fine specimen too. Harmony pretty nearly crushed the critter's skull and broke his leg. I never saw a horse do so much damage. We thought you'd want to have the wolf tanned and mounted."

Margaret turned her eyes away from the furry gray bundle. "You keep it, Jake. You killed it."

Jake said Mr. Lennox had shot it and if Margaret didn't want the skin he'd like it for the wall of his new house. Margaret raised her eyes inquiringly. As he gave her his cup for more coffee Mr. Lennox told her about the new ranch house he was going to build in the spring, natural wood with an enormous fireplace in the living room and one wall a window that would bring the prairie right into the house. He and Jake were already collecting stones for the fireplace. Doc had given him a petrified dinosaur's egg as big as a child's football. That was going in and anything else interesting that he could find.

Margaret took down the Custer rifle and showed it to him. Jake had not seen it and the two men examined it curiously.

"I don't suppose you would sell it to me to put over the fireplace?" Mr. Lennox asked hesitantly. "But of course you wouldn't. I really shouldn't ask."

"I'm afraid not. It's a gift. Pat found it and gave it to me." As he returned the gun to her their fingers met. Pat wondered why Margaret glowed, but not for long; she was eager to ask Mr. Lennox when he was going to bring his show horses to the ranch.

"I had intended to before this," he told her, "but Lady Luck has a cold and I've been afraid to move her. Now I'll have to wait until spring. Did you know she won a couple of firsts in the American Royal?"

"How proud you must be." Margaret served another piece of

cake. "Tell me more about the house. Are you going to use cottonwood?"

Pat took her cake in her hand and beckoned to Jake.

"Let's go tell Harmony about the wolf. I think he ought to have an extra lump of sugar."

She and Jake went out behind the corral and whistled for Harmony who came prancing across the meadow.

"Well, champ," Jake said, rubbing the horse's nose. "Pretty proud of yourself? That wolf was after the sheep, but he might have hamstrung you the way he did your mother. I bet you, Pat, a horse has a longer memory than an elephant."

"I know it." Pat threw her arms around the horse's neck. "You can laugh, but when Harmony was looking after that wolf, quivering all over and snorting and gleaming wet, I could feel him remembering. He was remembering being a little colt in the dark, rubbing against his mother, and smelling the wolf smell and his mother's shriek when the wolf fastened on her. I heard a horse scream once. And he remembered how terrified he was running farther away from that smell, scratching himself on the bushes in the dark, lost and weak and terribly afraid. No wonder his nerves were jerking—I could feel them under my hand."

She rubbed Harmony's neck and he snuffed in her pocket for sugar. She gave him two lumps.

"Harmony, honey, I'm so proud of you I could flap my wings and crow," she said softly.

The next morning on the way to school Pat and Margaret passed Ed Lancaster and one of his hands putting a ring of picket fence around a haystack. Ed came over and spoke to them, dabbing with a bandanna at his cold red nose.

"High time we put the hay fences up before the cattle get at the stacks. You'd better send that horse out coyote hunting. Think of the money you'd make in bounties."

Pat beamed. And so it was, everyone they saw had heard about Harmony. Mrs. Johnson wanted to know all about it when she brought Johnny, Ruby and Eric to school, and so did Mr. Yates. They talked so long that Margaret was fifteen minutes late ringing the bell.

Bob was almost as proud of Harmony as was Pat herself. That Saturday as they pulled tumbleweed from the fences nearest the house they speculated about how they could build some proper jumps. Bob had never seen them, but his father had brought him a souvenir program of the American Royal show at Kansas City which he had attended once when he drove a bunch of cattle to the stockyards. And Bob's uncle had ridden in the cutting-horse contests in the same show, so he felt that in a way he was an authority.

He and Pat liked to clean out the tumbleweed which, if it were left, stuck in the wire to form a solid wall and hold snowdrifts. Especially on a day when there was a little wind, these grayish-brown balls that looked at close hand like the delicate skeletons of clustered flowers, scurried across the prairie as though they were a herd of fluffy little animals.

Everything was urgent these days. No time to dawdle, even to train the horses before the snow came. The Saturday afternoon before Thanksgiving, after she had worked all morning, Pat rode over to Ty Chisholm's to see if Doc was there. He had been away; always in the late fall he went East for several weeks to hunt and see the horse shows. She found him with Jake in the corral. He had just come from the show in Madison Square Garden and told Pat about a young Mexican girl, barely nineteen, who had won a flock of ribbons.

"She's had more experience in jumping than you have, of course, but she doesn't ride any better."

Doc promised to come over one afternoon and see how she and Harmony had progressed, and it would be soon because everybody predicted an early winter. Before he left he called Pat to his pickup and gave her a round drumlike package wrapped in heavy paper.

"Open it and see how its fits."

Pat tugged at the paper, so eager to see what was inside that she had difficulty in untying the string. She uncovered a small hatbox with a bright hunting scene running around it, a green lane, hounds, riders in pink coats, and on the top the name of a famous New York sports shop. She untied the tapes and took off the lid. In a nest of tissue paper was a black hunting cap with a tiny bow of ribbon in the back and a flat button on top.

"It's what the gals are wearing in the ring. I thought it would be more becoming to you than a derby. Put it on. Let's see how it fits. No, not on the back of your head, pull it farther over your eyes."

Pat climbed into the car and looked at herself in the mirror— at the hazel eyes set wide apart, the snip of a nose and the mouth that was too large. The face didn't seem to her worthy of this marvelous cap.

"Do I look all right?" she asked anxiously.

"As sweet as the *señorita* I was telling you about. We must begin to collect your gear. Next spring you're going to be needing it. I'd have brought you boots if I'd known the size."

"Oh, Doc!" Pat sighed. "Oh, Doc!"

"There, there now, you look as though you were going to cry. That's no way to receive a present. But be tactful, my dear, when you show it to your mother."

Pat rode home slowly, holding the box before her. She put it on the top shelf of her closet and laid the cap on her bed. When Margaret came home from Strool, Pat showed it to her.

"What a pretty little cap. Too bad it's black. It would be more becoming if it were red or blue."

Margaret didn't know it was a hunting cap. Pat carried it

back into her room, wrapped it in the tissue paper and put it
away in the box. Was it wrong not to tell Mummy why Doc
gave it to her? All evening she thought about it, but could not
bring herself to say anything. Since her mother had accepted
Harmony after he killed the wolf, even seemed fond of him, it
would be wicked to disturb the peace between them.

So Pat said nothing, and uneasily watched the snow that
drifted by the window. In the morning it had stopped but it was
too deep for the Ford to plow through, even with a shovel in the
car. When Pat went out to feed the chickens the wind was
whipping the snow slantwise like a barrage, plastering her eyelashes and cutting her face. She and Margaret tied wool kerchiefs over their heads, put on extra pairs of wool stockings and
started to school. The wind was at their backs, it pushed them
along as though they were tumbleweed, sometimes faster than
they could walk so that they stumbled and went down on their
knees. But it exhilarated them, made them feel as strong as
giants.

Margaret's hands were so numb that she could scarcely make
the fire. Pat stayed in the basement with her until they were
thawed out. Soon the children came, the Johnsons in an old
sleigh with straw in it. There was a great stamping of boots in
the hall and shaking of snow from scarves and hoods.

The snow stayed on until after Christmas. There was not
much visiting during the holidays; Doc rode over with a brace
of pheasants for Margaret, and Ed Lancaster brought her a
haunch of venison. She and Ma Chisholm spent their afternoons
on the phone, it was their church and their club, when neighbors joined in they knew who had a sore throat or when the
new baby was expected. Every incident of family life took on a
heightened interest. Although they didn't say so to each other,
Pat and Margaret missed the box of sometimes useless but always glamorous presents that used to come from Sketch. Pat

was glad when school opened again, even though it meant coming home to a bitter cold house and wearing her coat and mittens until the kitchen fire burned up.

Ed Lancaster had taken down the fences around the haystacks and sheep were nibbling at the stack in the hay meadow,
eating it around the bottom so that it began to hang over like a
thatched roof. Harmony had his own hay, a loft full of it; no
matter what the weather, Pat managed to throw it down for
him and keep his stall filled with fresh straw. When the wind
was bitter he stayed in the stable or on the lee side of the barn
where the sheep huddled. They were stupid creatures, the
sheep, and never thought for themselves, just endured. When a
storm caught them it pushed them into a fence corner and there
they bunched, their heads down, their backs to the wind. Unless somebody drove them to shelter they would stand dumbly
and let themselves be buried; a nubbly white mound would be
all that was left of them.

When there was no wind to hide it with a stinging, whirling
curtain, the prairie gleamed with enchanted beauty, rippling
on and on as though it were spread with a carelessly tucked
coverlet of white satin. The gray logs of the house looked black,
at a little distance even Harmony looked black. The only color
in this black and white world was Pat's red kerchief which
made such a bright spot that she felt like an Indian signal fire.

In January the blizzard hit. All night it snowed, falling on
an old layer several inches deep. By morning it was still coming
down in such fine whirling flakes that Pat could scarcely find
her way to the barn.

"We can't see where we're going," she told Margaret. "Don't
you think we should ride Harmony?"

Margaret had been looking out the window. She agreed that
it was the only thing to do; a horse can pick his way when
humans can't. So they ducked their heads and ran blindly to the

stable. Pat saddled Harmony, sprang on and waited for Margaret to climb up behind her. Sheltered by Pat's shoulder, Margaret could perhaps see the road. But Harmony didn't lose it. When Pat turned him into the schoolyard he was blowing a little, so exhausting had been those two miles. She rode him into the shed and hitched him to the rail. By the time the fire was started the other children came.

"If it keeps up, we're going to have a hard time getting you out," Mr. Yates said as he deposited Nancy and Alec in the vestibule. "But my kids like to come. They wouldn't stay at home."

It did keep up; by noon the wind was driving the snow with such fury that no truck could find a way through it, nor could a horse. The children could not go out to play; they ate their lunches huddling around the register. Margaret drew a donkey on the blackboard and they took turns blindfolding each other and trying to draw a tail on it. By three o'clock when school should have been out, they were as restless as a stableful of colts in March, but the wind was blowing the snow so hard that they couldn't see through the window. "We'll have to stay here all night," Margaret thought, appalled. "Whatever shall I do with them!" Physically she was prepared for such an emergency, groceries on the shelves in the basement, a couple of stew pans, even nine plates and cups and saucers, knives, forks and spoons, but she had not imagined how hard it would be to keep the children entertained. If she gave them hot soup that would consume a little time. Bob and Pat offered to help; they opened two cans and heated them on the furnace. The children thought it was a picnic, they drank the soup from the cups and spooned out the vegetables, scattering cracker crumbs. Bob had a way with children; he took charge and Margaret let him, pleased to find masculine strength to lean on. Eric, he decreed, and Ruby should take a nap. He spread coats and scarves on the floor near the radiator and wrapped them up.

"When you wake," he promised, "we'll play a new game that

I've made up." For the others he arranged a dishwashing and floor-sweeping brigade. He would have liked to go to the shed to see the horses, but the wind was blowing so hard that he was afraid he would let in an avalanche of snow if he opened the door. As the open side of the shed was to the lee of the wind, he knew the horses were protected by the warm-packed drift.

By the time Eric and Ruby awoke it was dark. Margaret lit the two big oil lamps with the tin reflectors that sat in brackets on the wall. They made a pleasant yellow glow. Bob, as good as his word, had thought of a game. He pushed the desks against the wall and in the cleared room gathered the children. He had found in his coat pocket a piece of rope which he had fashioned into a noose.

"I'm a cowboy," he said, "and you are cattle. Pat, blindfold me. I'm going to lasso you and the one I catch is 'it.' See, all I have to do is to put this noose over your head."

Margaret behind her desk sat in the only safety zone watching the children mill and scream with laughter. Bob caught Ruby; she giggled as Pat tied the kerchief over her eyes. How long, Margaret wondered desperately, could they keep this up? If only they would play until suppertime. She felt as wooden as a totem pole, not an idea in her head, loathing herself for her inadequacy, dreading the long night. She leaned her head on her hands and blessed Bob for his ingenuity; he kept them entertained until they were hungry and it was time to wash their hands and faces.

"What shall we have for supper?" Margaret asked. "We'll take a vote on it. We have baked beans and lima beans and spaghetti with tomato sauce." Spaghetti won. They heated several cans with the children standing around the furnace and sniffing the delightful smell. But with all the delay she could contrive, washing the dishes and cleaning the tomato sauce from Eric's face, when they came back upstairs it was only seven o'clock. "Now is the long stretch when they will get homesick and want their parents," Margaret thought in a panic. She sent Pat and Bob down to stoke the furnace—luckily there was plenty of coal—and when they came back she was showing Eric how to draw a cow. Ruby was scowling at a picture book that Margaret had found for her. The child's lips trembled.

"I want to go home," she sobbed. "I want my Mommy."

Pat wiped away a big tear that was trembling on the edge of the child's fat cheek.

"I know what let's do, we can play cowboy-at-a-roundup. We'll all sit around the campfire and tell stories." She brought in the coats from the vestibule and spread them in a wide circle around the register.

"Come on, Mummy, you begin. Tell us about the time Grandma took you to Pierre when you were a little girl; and how you were more than a week on the trail, sleeping in the wagon and cooking on a campfire. And how you met the Indian who gave you the eagle feather."

Bob took down one of the lamps from the wall and put it on Margaret's desk, to make it look like a campfire.

"Come on, Mrs. Cole. You start off. I know a good story that happened to my dad."

Margaret began hesitantly at first, but as she glanced from one to the other of the faces, in the yellow glow of the lamp, and knew that she must hold them, she began to remember the exact phrases that she had once repeated night after night for Pat. They came easily; before she had gotten to the Indian with the eagle feather Eric was nodding and Ruby asleep with her head buried in her long bright curls. Pat unbuttoned Ruby's shoes, slipped them off and folded her scarf for a pillow. The child curled up in a ball, like a kitten. Eric's boots were harder to pull off, but he was too sound asleep to care.

Bob hung the lamp on the wall again, then turned down both lamps.

"I'll tell my yarn in the dark and any cowboy who wants to hit the hay can just roll over and shut his eyes. One time when Daddy first came to this country and was building a soddy on Elk Creek," his voice had lowered into a drowsy singsong.

"He's practically talking them to sleep," Margaret thought. "How did he ever learn so much about children?"

Presently they were all asleep, even Pat and Bob. Margaret sat very still, listening to the wind and watching the turmoil of snow that fell past the window. Sometimes she dropped off to sleep; when she was wakened by the cold, she went to the basement and stoked the fire. Once Bob was awake and did it for her.

"It's easing off," he said. "Maybe in the morning they'll get through to us."

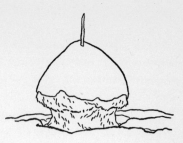

Chapter 11

Rescue

The next time Margaret opened her eyes it was morning; the wind had died, the snow was no longer falling and the sun was coming in through the drifts on the windowpane. The children began to waken and ran to the window to look out on the glistening world.

"It's drifting clear to the top of the shed," they cried. "We'll have to dig our way out of the door." They danced with excitement.

"Wait until we've had breakfast," Margaret said, "and we'll see what we can do before it's time for school."

On the furnace, Pat and Jane thawed water to wash their faces. Nancy Yates combed Ruby's curls, wrapping them around her finger. She scrubbed the child and smoothed her mussed pinafore; it was as much fun as playing with a doll.

"Ya, ya," shouted her contemptuous brother, Alec, "you always want to play house. I'm going out and make a snowman."

Margaret looked at her supplies, opened a box of quick oatmeal and punched holes in several cans of evaporated milk. The children ate the cereal while it was steaming hot. As soon as they had finished, Bob took the coal shovel upstairs and tried to open the outer door, but it would not budge. Margaret pushed; they all pushed. At last they moved it far enough for him to get the shovel through. The snow had drifted about half-way up. He did not attempt to push it wider, but dug a narrow pathway across the entrance and down the steps. Margaret helped and so did the children, even baby Eric stood on tiptoe and manfully pushed handfuls of snow over the top of the drifts.

On the ground it was only knee deep. Going very slowly and lifting his knees almost to his chin, Bob made his way to the shed. Pat followed, stepping in the holes that he had made. Harmony, Cindy, and Jane's pony had been snug enough, protected from the wind by the wall of snow drifted against the shed. There was no hay for them or water, but they would eat snow and when they were set loose they would paw their way to the grass even through this deep snow. Pat rubbed Harmony's face with her mitten. His coat was rough and shaggy; now she was glad she had not been able to keep him curried since it had been so cold. The horses stepped gingerly into the yard, their feet leaving deep, round holes like the burrows of small animals.

While Pat and Bob were returning, stepping in their own footprints to save the exertion of making new ones, they heard a buzzing in the still sky and saw Mr. Lennox's plane swooping down over them so low that it almost cut off the school-house chimney.

"Look, it's on skis!" Bob exclaimed. Mr. Lennox pushed back the top to lean out and wave. Then he tossed something down— a can that punched a hole in the snow not more than a few feet from where the children stood. Bob scrambled for it. Inside was a note:

Telephone wires down. If you need help, hang out a coat where we can see it. We'll be back.

They looked up. The plane did not circle again; already it was a speck over Strool.

Pat and Bob carried the note to Margaret who pinned it on the blackboard where everyone could see it. The children clamored to go out, hoping they would be allowed to watch for the plane's return.

"It's too deep," Bob said, "but they can come out on the stoop and in the little tunnel that we've cleared."

Whooping and laughing, the children put on their coats and mittens, ran out the door and began to dig into the walls of the tunnel. They grabbed handfuls of snow and scrubbed each other's faces, tumbling and rolling about, swallowing great mouthfuls, getting it in their eyes.

Bob shoveled to clear the entrance so he could open the door a little farther. Margaret came to the edge of the stoop and rang the bell. Alec Yates, playful as a bear cub in the spring, hopped onto the stoop and grabbed the handle of the shovel. Bob yanked it back to keep it out of the way of the other children coming up the steps. Alec pulled harder; Bob twisted; Alec yanked. . . . In the tussle, Bob tripped over the shovel and fell on the smaller boy. Alec hit the floor with a scream and lay there without attempting to get up, sobbing and groaning. Bob, who had struggled to his feet, lifted Alec from where he lay on the edge of the step with his arm twisted under him. Margaret, who had run to the door, saw Alec's forearm dangling, broken, with one end of the fractured bone sticking through the skin. She helped Bob carry him into the schoolhouse and lay him on the floor.

"Hold still," Margaret commanded. She was trembling so, that she could scarcely control her voice. "Bob, run to the basement and find me a piece of kindling as long and smooth as you can, without any splinters. Pat, get the first-aid kit and take out the bandage. Please, Alec, hold still." As gently as she could, trying to close her ears to his screams, she pulled the forearm until the bone was in place, then bound it against the piece of wood.

"Shall I hang out a coat?" Without waiting for an answer Bob took Alec's coat and hung it on the offending shovel before the door.

The two men looked like giants.

"Bob, I appoint you and Pat to hear the lessons. Pat, take Ruby and Eric, and Bob, Jane, Johnny and Nancy."

Bob and Pat set about it, hearing the lessons at a furious pace to keep the children so busy that they could not think about Alec. Margaret sat by the boy, holding his hand, mopping his tears and praying that Jake would come soon. While the first grade was drawing letters on their slates, Pat came over to her mother and whispered, "Let me stay with him. I'll keep him quiet." But Margaret shook her head. She was responsible for the accident—somehow she should have prevented it—now all that she could do was to make him as comfortable as possible. So she sat on, waiting and listening. It was a couple of hours before she heard the whir of the plane. She could not see it glide down on its skis for it landed in front of the schoolhouse,

but her sharpened ears told her when it taxied on the snow and
when the engine was cut off.

The two men stood in the doorway so wrapped in mufflers
that they looked like giants and seemed to fill the whole room
with their presence.

"Here we are, the winged St. Bernards. All we lack is a flask
around our necks. What can we do for you?" Mr. Lennox who
had never been inside the schoolhouse looked about with curios-
ity. Jake pushed past him and leaned over Alec.

"The Yates boy. Is it a bad break? Do you want us to take
him home or fly him to Bison to the doctor?"

"He needs a doctor. It's a fracture." Margaret climbed to her
feet and held out a hand to each of them. "Thank God for both
of you. I was desperate."

Mr. Lennox looked around for something to make a sling and
took Pat's kerchief which was large enough to knot behind the
boy's neck. They lifted him to his feet and cradled his arm in it.

"We're going to take you for a ride in the plane."

"Oh, gee!" Alec's tears stopped and although he winced when
he moved he looked at the others with a superior grin. As they
put on his ear muffs, cap and muffler and wrapped his coat
around him as best they could, Mr. Lennox told Margaret about
their reconnaissance flight. Old Mrs. Johnson had an attack of
appendicitis so they flew her to the hospital and on the way
back picked up Doc to attend Tom Schultz's prize bull.

"So we're practically a flying ambulance." He pressed Margaret's hand. "You're not to worry. We'll get the boy to Bison
and fly his mother to him."

Jake lifted Alec and carried him to the plane. The children
huddled in the doorway to watch the take-off. They did not
want to go back to their lessons and Margaret could not hold
their attention. She was glad when it was noon and they could
go down to the basement to heat beans. While they were eating
they heard a great clanking on the road. Everybody rushed up-

stairs to look out the door. It was Mr. Yates in the caterpillar tractor that belonged to the Department of Highways. He waved as he drew up at a spot where the ends of the fence posts marked the gate.

Did he know about Alec? Margaret felt a choking sensation in her throat. She couldn't say a word; she waited for him to speak.

"They got Alec to Bison all right. He's home now, fixed up in a cast. Don't you have him on your mind, Mrs. Cole. These things will happen and you surely did the best you could." Margaret swallowed hard and gave him a grateful smile. The snowplow, Mr. Yates said, would not be through for hours, probably not for days, but he would take Margaret and the four younger children home on the tractor if they would all promise to stick on tight. Pat, Bob and Jane could ride in the path they broke.

With whoops of excitement the children ran to get their coats. Margaret tied up their ears and saw that their mittens were pulled on. Pat, Bob and Jane went out into the yard to catch the horses.

Harmony, Cindy and the pony danced along impatiently behind the tractor and the bundled children sitting on top of its hump. While it was not as exciting as a plane ride, they were making the most of the adventure. Where the road passed the Cole ranch the tractor went on and the riders had to break their own paths through the snow. This was slow work. Bob went first, letting Cindy take her time. Where the path to the Lancaster ranch branched off at the gate of the hay meadow he and Jane waved good-by. Pat wasn't far from the barn now. Luckily, the gate to the corral had been left open. Before she went into the house Pat put Harmony in his stall and threw down a good meal of hay. Tip ran into the stall, barking and wagging his ridiculous little tail. After Harmony had nuzzled him, the pup followed Pat to the house. She had lighted the kitchen fire and stood shivering over it, trying to warm her hands.

"You poor little starved thing. You shall have something to eat just as soon as I get thawed out."

By the time Mr. Yates brought Margaret home on the tractor, Pat had a hot fire going and a pot of coffee on the stove. Mr. Yates came in, with Margaret, to warm his hands. While they both stood close to the stove, Pat poured the coffee. They were too cold to leave the stove so they drank it standing and ate the cookies she brought from the cookie jar. Finally Mr. Yates wiped the crumbs from his chapped mouth and pulled on his gloves with the sheepskin backs.

"I'll be getting along. Don't you worry about a thing. No use trying to keep school until next week when we'll have the road open. Have you everything you need?"

Margaret nodded, her lips still stiff with cold.

"I can't begin to thank you," Margaret said gratefully.

When she had closed the door Margaret began to cry, silently, trembling as though she had a chill. Pat dragged a chair to the fire, pushed her in it gently and gave her mother another cup of coffee.

"Everything's all right, Mummy. Honestly it is."

Margaret wiped her eyes with the fingers of her mittens.

"I know it is, dear. It's just that I'm so tired."

Chapter 12

The Gift

As soon as they had thawed their frozen bones, Pat and Margaret went out to see what had happened to the sheep. Now there was no wind and the sun, trying to break through the pale gray incandescent sky, was like a light in a frosted bulb. Pat turned her eyes from the tracks that led to the road and barn and looked toward the buttes where not even a rabbit had made a footprint in the snow. The only living thing was the eagle that nested on a ledge of one of the sheer cliffs; it was making a reconnaissance, sailing in a wide circle and throwing a blue shadow on the snow. How clean the prairie looked, she thought, as if God had just finished making it.

"We can't stay out long." Margaret pulled her scarf tighter around her ears. They could see as far as the creek where the black limbs of the cottonwoods were edged with white and the willows bent under their weight of snow. The sheep weren't there, unless they were buried altogether. Slowly, lifting their knees, they waded to the far side of the barn and sheds which were hidden from the house. There were the sheep, a large group of them huddled against the side of the buildings, motionless in a tight-packed, dirty, gray splotch, half buried even though they were protected from the drifts. Margaret ran an appraising eye over them.

"That's not all. There are some by the fence of the feed yard. Let's put hay out for them until we clear a path and get them into the sheds. They can't walk through this snow, it's above their knees."

The stacks of hay in the feed yard, which looked like fat loaves of iced cake, were so buried in snow that it would take some time to dig one out; and already their fingers were stiff. It was easier to take the hay from the barn. Harmony neighed when they passed his stall and stuck out his head to rub Pat's sleeve.

"You've had your dinner, boy." She hugged him before she climbed into the loft and began to pitch down hay, as much as she could lift. Margaret carried armloads of it to the sheep. When they smelled it they lifted their heads, shook the snow from their flanks and stretched out their necks tentatively, like old women putting their hands out of the window to see how cold it is.

"That's enough. Come on down," Margaret called. "Let's get in before our ears freeze." Pat slid awkwardly down the ladder, her feet numb; they clumped back to the kitchen, walking in their tracks.

In the kitchen, Pat thrust more wood into the stove, which already was glowing red hot. They stood close to it, holding out their hands, putting first one foot in the oven, then the other, and turning to thaw out their icy backs. The kitchen was so warm and cozy that it made them feel drowsy and contented. They smiled at each other as though they had come home after a long and exhausting journey. Margaret moved first, shook herself a little, took off her scarf and boots and said it was time to get supper. From the cupboard she brought a piece of ham that had been left from Sunday. One last jar of beans was on the shelf and some cold potatoes that she could fry. In the morn-

ing they would have to break a path to the soddy. Pat set the
table, using her grandmother's silver spoons instead of the tin
ones from the kitchen drawer.

"Mummy, just once couldn't I have some coffee and drink it
out of a wedding ring cup?"

Margaret twitched Pat's ear.

"All right, chick, just this once. You want to celebrate?" She
stirred the potatoes, which were beginning to brown; their
aroma filled the kitchen, mixed with the fresh, delicate scent of
vegetables starting to boil.

At supper Pat drank her coffee slowly. She didn't really like
it, but it was a symbol, it meant being grown-up, so she sipped
it until she could see the gold ring in the bottom of the cup.

"Mummy, I've got a problem," she said. "Do you think you
could help me?"

Margaret who had been trying to estimate in her mind how
many of the sheep were missing, looked up absently.

"I might if it isn't too serious. What is it?"

"Well, it's Doc. Next month is his birthday, February twenty-
second, the same as Washington's. I thought I'd like to give him
a birthday present, but I don't know what it would be."

"That takes some thought," Margaret admitted. "Let's see."
It was much more cheerful thinking about a present for Doc
than counting your losses from the storm and wondering how
you were going to get along next summer. "We might as well
wash the dishes while we're thinking."

Pat got up reluctantly, she felt so lazy that she would have
liked to crawl under the stove and purr like a cat. When they
had put away the dishes and hung up the tea towel on the line
behind the stove, Margaret got out her knitting; she had un-
raveled one of Sketch's sweaters, a gay red one, and was making it over for Pat. Pat's old one was so small that it left a cold
midriff when she wore it over jeans and the sleeves were half-
way to the elbows.

"Now about the present. Have we anything that would do?"

Pat brought her treasure box from her room and set it on the kitchen table—a smoothly-sanded cigar box from which Sketch had scraped the label. The dovetailing at the corners made an attractive pattern of light and dark. Sketch had waxed it until it glowed; inside, Margaret had glued a satin lining.

The firelight was being blotted up by the dark. Margaret switched on the light. Unwrapping a bit of tissue paper Pat laid her first treasure on the cloth—a little gold lucky charm that Sketch had carried in his pocket. Looking at it Pat could see him leaping out of a chute on a plunging bronc, a flash of resplendent color in his cream beaver Stetson, his white satin shirt, tight blue jeans and black boots with a slash of red at the top. No, she couldn't give away the charm, it was a part of him. She rewrapped it and laid it aside.

There was the little brass horse sharply cut, with one foot raised, a high-action trotter, but this was a girl's pin; Sketch had brought it for her to wear on the lapel of the green suede suit he sent her from Kansas City. The ring with her birthstone in it, the cross on its fine gold chain, the necklace of gilt leaves that was as flexible as a snake—she pushed them all aside.

Margaret had been watching as her fingers moved over and under with the knitting.

"Did you find anything?"

"No, I didn't." Pat refilled the box and tied a narrow ribbon around it. "They're all for girls."

"Then, let's see what I have." Margaret thrust her needles through the sweater and brought from her bedroom a similar box.

"Patsy," she said as she opened the lid, "you know if we had the money you could have it to buy Doc a present, don't you?" She put out her hand and pushed back the hair that always seemed to escape Pat's braids like a cloud of pale down. "I just don't dare spend a cent for I'm not sure how we're going to get through the year."

Pat rubbed her cheek against her mother's sleeve. The wool scratched a little and it felt warm like a caress.

"Of course, I understand, Mummy, and I'm going to help somehow."

Margaret brushed her lips across Pat's forehead.

"Don't worry, we'll get along. I just wanted you to know. Now let's see. I've almost forgotten what's here."

An old garnet star-shaped brooch that had belonged to Pat's grandmother; she had brought it from Pennsylvania. A blue enamel locket with a seed pearl set in the middle of a little gold bow; so old that Margaret couldn't remember to whom it had belonged—some aunt, perhaps, whom she had never seen; but the nicks, according to her mother, were made by her own baby teeth. A stickpin with a tiny diamond in it. Margaret held it out to Pat who twirled it in the light.

"May I have that? It's beautiful."

Margaret considered it for a long time, then took it back from Pat and laid it aside. It had belonged to her father and Pat was welcome to it, but somehow she was afraid it wasn't the sort of thing men wore nowadays. A pair of earrings, little mosaic flowers that Sketch had found; a pair of gold cuff links, they might have done but one of the links was broken.

"What's this, Mummy?" Pat lifted out a gold bar about an inch long, with a hook on it and hanging from it was a stiff brown-plaited band.

"That? It's what's left of a watch fob. Men used to wear them in their waistband pockets. When your grandfather still lived in Pennsylvania he had a trotting horse of whom he was very fond and when the horse won a prize at the State Fair he had that horsehair fob made. See, it's from King Cole's tail."

Horsehair, something from Harmony's tail! Doc would like

that, but what could he use? What did men wear nowadays that could be made of horsehair? They both racked their brains but could think of nothing. However, Margaret kept out the watch fob in case they had an idea.

"Of course," she said, "you could always give him a birthday dinner, he likes parties."

Pat agreed that the dinner would have to do if she couldn't think of anything else. She could make a belt but she could never get enough horsehair; she couldn't pull out all of Harmony's tail. But why not a buckle? She could cover one with horsehair by crocheting it tight and it would look different and interesting. Margaret agreed that Doc would be amused. In the morning she would look for an old buckle that she had saved from a coat belt.

Not long after breakfast the next morning, Ed Lancaster and Bob rode up. They had been looking for their cattle. Ed was afraid there would be heavy losses among the cattle for they did not graze near the ranch houses; but most of the sheep, he thought, were safe since they had been in the corrals. He and Bob shoveled a path for the sheep behind the barn and the feed lot, and drove them into the sheds.

"Not too many missing," he said after he and Margaret had counted them. "I make it not more than six. Bob and I will dig out one of the haystacks. Do you think you and Pat can manage to pitch them hay? Bob will be able to help some." Margaret was sure they could; she and Pat waved them good-by and watched the two figures riding slowly across the prairie, the rumps of their horses sticking up broad and dark above the snow.

Pat had tried out the idea of the buckle on Bob and he had been so pleased with it that he wanted to make one himself; so during the long January evenings after her lessons were done, Pat worked on the gift. It wasn't difficult to get enough horsehair; Harmony didn't mind having it pulled from his tail. He enjoyed being groomed and considered this part of his toilet. As there was no chance to brush and comb him on these bitter days he switched his tail invitingly every time Pat came to the barn. But most of the time she had just come to get the pitchfork on her way to pitching hay for the sheep. They were so dingy gray and grubby, she hated cleaning their sheds. Taking care of Harmony's stall was different; even with the thermometer hovering at zero she kept it fresh and clean. It gave her a sense of accomplishment to pitch down his hay for he was filling out, his hip bones didn't stick up any more and he was as plump as one could want a horse to be.

When she came into the house Pat always found plenty of hot water on the stove. Margaret didn't want people to say her daughter always smelled of the stable; but she knew it was difficult for Pat to keep changing jeans every time she did the chores, so she could not be too critical. She was grateful that Pat had taken the responsibility of the sheep. Margaret was beginning to lean on Pat and now she did not feel so terribly alone. To be sure the decisions were hers, the worries about making both ends meet, but in their daily living Pat had become a partner. Winter, with its harsh demands, was bringing them closer together.

Pat, too, felt this change in the atmosphere and bloomed. To be helping, to be appreciated and praised instead of feeling like a rebellious outcast living under the shadow of Margaret's disapproval, gave the girl a zest that sometimes was almost overwhelming. Margaret was unable to think of enough chores to keep her occupied.

Not even the horsehair buckle ate up all her energy although it took longer than she had expected. It was forever pulling crooked and getting kinks and bulges. Horsehair was slippery stuff and many an evening she took out almost as much as she wove. By the beginning of February she was not more than half done. There seemed to be so little time, what with Lincoln's

birthday and Valentine's day to celebrate at school, and helping Margaret collect red and white paper for valentines and
making designs simple enough for the children to cut out.

Pat had not seen Doc since he had brought the pheasants at
Christmas. The week before his birthday the buckle was done
but it didn't look impressive enough, not alone, so she decided
to invite him to dinner. When she phoned, his housekeeper
answered and said he had been in bed with the flu. She suggested that the dinner come to him.

"You bring whatever you want and heat it on my stove. It
will be good for him to have company."

So on the twenty-second, Pat took a basket of Southern fried
chicken and all the trimmings, starting soon after she finished
the morning chores for it was sixteen miles to Strool. The sun
was out and the snow melting; Harmony's hoofs made squidges
in the soft mud. Every chunk that splattered the saddle grieved
her. This was the first time she had used it since the bad
weather, but she felt this long ride was a special occasion. The
ranches looked much larger and more important than when she
had come to Strool in a car; the billows of the prairie, gray now
with the melting snow, seemed higher. Harmony arched his
neck and pranced. When a truck passed, the only one they met
on the road, he shied playfully and nearly upset the basket.

Presently the village appeared a long way off—a crossroads
and ten or twelve houses. As Pat came nearer she could recognize the church. Doc's house was only a step beyond. She eased
the basket down to the porch, took Harmony to the stable and
gave him his oats. Doc's housekeeper met her at the door, a
jolly buxom woman with one tooth missing. She kept putting
her tongue in the space when she smiled.

"Come on, honey, Doc's expecting you. Why don't you go on
in and see him and I'll heat up the dinner. When it's ready I'll
call you and you can help serve it."

Doc was in the sitting room close to the fire, wrapped in a

heavy wool dressing gown, his feet on a hassock and a rug over his knees.

"Come in, my dear. Forgive me for not getting up. That woman has me swaddled like a month-old baby, but I'll admit it does feel comfortable. Take off your coat and come over to the fire."

This was the first time Pat had seen Doc's house. She looked at the pictures above the fireplace: Doc as a young man on a fine tall horse with a pack of hounds around him, the same horse with Doc up, skimming a brush jump with his feet folded under him clean and neat, and Doc holding the bridle of the horse on which a judge was pinning a ribbon.

"That's Pluto," Doc said, following Pat's eyes. "He was black as soot and one of the best hunters that ever took a wall. My father gave him to me when I was sixteen and he had been hunting only one season. We grew up together. After I came back from the war I began to take him to the shows. He won everything in Maryland and Virginia and I was planning to take him to Madison Square Garden when he broke his leg on a ditch. And it was my fault, I was so proud of him that I let my captain ride him on a hunt. He forced Pluto to take the ditch when the horse knew better. It had been raining, the ground was soft, and the bank didn't hold. Pat, when I had to shoot that horse I was sick for a week."

Pat stared at the pictures, she didn't dare look at Doc for fear the tears in her eyes would run over.

"There, there, honey," he said, patting her hand, "it was a long time ago."

Pat fumbled in her pocket and laid the horsehair buckle on his lap, trying not to think of Pluto. She was shy about the gift and embarrassed, remembering all the mistakes she had made.

Doc undid the tissue paper and put on his glasses.

"It's Harmony's hair. I thought maybe you'd like it."

"My dear, I love it. I'll keep it for my best belt. When Harmony wins his first blue ribbon I'll be just as proud of him as you are."

"Do you think he will, Doc, really?"

Doc looked her straight in the eyes, he was not fooling her, he meant it when he said Harmony might well turn out to be as fine a horse as Pluto.

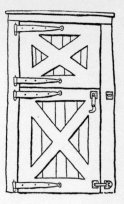

Chapter 13

Officially Spring

The minute the frost was out of the ground Mr. Lennox planned to start his new barn, then the house on the knoll above Ty's place. Whenever she could, Pat rode by to watch the supplies piling up in the sheds, truckloads of cement and bolts and iron beams. Early in April when Jake was going to Rapid City on a Saturday he offered to take her along. In the morning, when she stuck her head out of the window to see what kind of day it was, the wind was chilly. When she walked down to the road the sun had come out. The ground was a sponge, soft as dough; she felt as though it wouldn't hold her up. Melting snow running into the creeks made a faint rustling music; the whole air was singing; even the faded brown prairie stirred, getting ready for spring.

Pat saw Jake a long way off, the red truck kicking up sprays of mud. He gave her a hand up and they rattled along, slithering about but not minding for they had the whole road to themselves. As they rolled along, passing occasional ranches and groups of cattle looking up stolidly from their feeding, Jake told Pat that in the fall he and Lily would be married. He liked to talk things over with her; it was like talking to himself except better, a way of clearing up his mind. During the summer he and Lily wanted to make over her father's old ranch house, paint it and put in a bath and hot water. Lily's father was a real old-timer, who had trapped in the country before it was opened up. He would be happy sleeping near the ashes of a campfire and eating out of a skillet; he thought it sissy to bathe in a white enameled tub, but Lily had been working on him and the thought of having someone to depend on for help with the stock reconciled him to change. In other ways his mind was not ossified.

"You should see that new calf he bought," Jake offered as proof, "a Scottish highland critter bred to withstand the cold. He has a ruff of fur around his neck that is so shaggy you could mistake him for a lion."

Pat was only half listening for this was going to be her year too, her's and Harmony's; in her imagination she was running so eagerly to meet the summer that she was unconscious of time or the gradual change to higher, bleaker ground with ranches farther apart, the land poorer, less inhabited. When they whizzed through Newell, a real town with feed and hardware stores and shops, she came out of her dream. They were climbing into hills, forested with pines, and sliding down toward Sturgis, an enchanted little white town in a valley. On their left, one butte stood out by itself, much higher than the others, bald and round as a sugar loaf.

"That's Bear Butte," Jake told her. "The Dakota Indians hold their pow-wows there once every year. It's a sacred mountain."

Pat looked at it with awe; it seemed lonesome and deserted now. Presently they began to pass tourist homes and signs pointing to "The Petrified Forest." This was the old, old land of her school history. In these caves were buried the forests that covered these hills thousands of years ago and here were found the fossils of saber-toothed tigers and three-toed horses. She wished she could go into one of them, but there wasn't time; as it was they wouldn't get home until after dark.

"Watch when we come into Rapid City," Jake said. "On the hills above the town they've built life-size statues of prehistoric animals. You'll see one that's a hundred feet long and as big as a house, with a head like a horse and a tail like a lizard. I don't know which one he is, maybe a dinosaur."

Pat watched for it. She stared at everything as they came into Rapid City: the railroad tracks, the houses so close together that one could call from one yard to another, the people on the streets, so many of them that she wondered what kept them from bumping into each other. On a ridge overlooking the town Jake pointed out the huge cement creatures.

"Makes you feel like a gnat, doesn't it? I guess they were just too big to be practical; must have sort o' got in their own way."

Jake parked on a side street and took Pat to lunch in a bright, crowded place with a counter and booths along the wall. Men in Stetsons, bright shirts and cowboy boots sat at the counter, but somehow they didn't look like cowboys, their hands were soft and their faces untanned and their hips were too thick. Pat whispered as much to Jake.

"Oh, they're just the local boys. They run the stores, the banks and such things. They're tame cats, but they all like to think of themselves as part of the big bad West. And they believe in advertising. They even like to have the Indians around, not only for their trade but because they give a bit of color. See that old Indian going by the window in his black Stetson with a couple of braids over his shoulder. He's probably going to the ten-cent store; nothing really exciting about him, but don't you like to look at him?"

Yes, she did, but there were so many more unusual things to look at—the bright cigarette machine and the jukebox topped with a picture of a white horse behind which a yellow light glowed. When someone put in a nickel, cascades of varicolored lights flooded the whole machine.

Pat's eyes lit on a hot fudge sundae, a beautiful concoction with its whipped cream topped with a cherry. It was being eaten by an old gentleman in black broadcloth with white hair that hung down to his collar. He, too, was wearing cowboy boots, and hanging on the rack behind him was a ten-gallon Stetson. When he saw Pat eying his dessert he smiled at her.

"You'll like it," he said. "Hello, Jake. How's your father?"

"Not too good, Judge, but he doesn't complain. Pat, I see one of my buddies at the bar. Will you be all right while I speak to him?"

"Of course, she will," said the Judge. "I'll sit with her." He brought his ice cream over to her table and when he unfolded he must have been nearly seven feet tall.

"Do you like it better with nuts on it or without?" he asked solemnly.

"I don't know. I've never tasted it."

"Then you must try it with nuts." He summoned the waitress with a lordly gesture.

"Not another sundae, Judge?" she asked in mock amazement.

"Certainly, another sundae and see that the fudge is hot. And this little lady will have one with both nuts and a cherry and an extra dollop of whipped cream. How do you feel?" he asked Pat solicitously. "Is your blood tingling and would you like to run from here to Kansas City? I've spring fever; I may paw the ground and neigh if I don't watch out. I'm tired of sitting in my office listening to people tell me their silly troubles. While young Jake loads up, let's go shopping; let's go to the movies, do something gay. We'll look for a doll, but I suppose you're too old to play with dolls. Too bad." He stuck his long finger in her face and thundered, "What do you play with?"

"Harmony," Pat answered, too startled to think of anything else.

"And what, may I ask, is harmony? I have never considered it a plaything."

Between bites of the delicious chocolate that stuck to her spoon and had to be licked off, Pat told the judge about Harmony; about the wolf that killed his mother and how he had kicked the other wolf to death. And how already he was a good jumper.

"Horse crazy, eh?" The judge blinked his solemn eyes at her. "When you let him out and go scorching across the prairie with the wind whipping your hair in your eyes and dust choking your throat, do you feel that you wouldn't change with the archangel Gabriel and sit on a golden throne? And when he gets a stone in his foot, do you freeze to the very marrow for fear he's going lame? Yes, of course, you do. I can see it in your eyes. My dear young lady, it's a disease, a plague, a curse, and you'll never get over it. However, there's a movie down the street in which, so they aver, there's good riding. I'll speak to Jake."

The judge stood up and took his ten-gallon hat off the peg. He moved with long, swinging strides like a giant in seven-league boots. Pat ate the last bit of her whipped cream with something like consternation. She saw Jake nod and a moment later the judge was standing over her; smiling not at her, but at something in his own mind—the smile of a mischievous, overgrown hobgoblin.

They went out onto the street. Everybody spoke to the judge; he kept sweeping off the black Stetson in a gesture that reminded Pat of the arm of a windmill. In the theater, the picture already had begun; they found their seats in the dark. The heroine was in the stable patting a black mare with a star on her face. The girl's red Technicolor shirt, the blue of her eyes and the gold of her curls were as sharp and exaggerated as the colors in a storybook. She looked so slicked up that Pat sniffed. "She isn't taking care of him herself. I bet she doesn't know how."

Presently the scene changed; the girl, in a black riding habit and a derby, came out upon the terrace of a great white house with two-story pillars, bigger and more beautiful than any that Pat had ever seen. A groom led the mare up the drive, her coat gleaming like satin. The girl mounted; she rode down the drive and next Pat saw her with a group of huntsmen and a pack of hounds just like those on her hatbox. They moved down a country lane shadowed with tall arching trees, such trees as Pat had only seen in books, and presently the camera left the other huntsmen and followed the girl and a young man. They rode along woods trails, across fields, jumping gates, stone fences and ditches. Pat held her breath, rising in her stirrups with the girl, sailing through the air, coming down with her calves tight against the ribs of the mare. She didn't listen to the story; she was too busy absorbing sensations with her eyes. The close-ups annoyed her. Why did they waste time talking? Why did the girl bat her eyelashes and look at the man as though she could claw his heart out, and why did he grab her and smother her with kisses? Pat wanted to get back to the horses; and finally the picture did.

Pimlico, the race track! She never had seen a race track. This must be a steeplechase about which Doc had told her; there were the poles and the brush, the coop and water jump. The trumpet blew, the crowds cheered. Again Pat identified herself with the girl on the screen. Each jump was higher or more difficult, worst of all was the water jump. Would the mare refuse? No, she was taking it. She had won! When the girl and the black mare faced the judges, Pat gave a sigh and closed her eyes. The tension was over; she felt herself falling back into the movie house, into the narrow seat with its little upholstered arm.

Blinking, Pat glanced at the illuminated clock on the left of the screen. Three-thirty; Jake would be waiting for her. Suddenly she remembered the judge. Glancing up at him apologetically, she caught her breath in relief; his eyes were closed, his chin sunk on his chest and his breath making little whistling noises in his throat. What should she do? She mustn't keep Jake waiting; she didn't like to climb over the judge. Two minutes, three minutes, the hands on the big electric clock crawled around. It had to be done, she put her hand out and gently touched the big one lying on his knee. The judge opened his eyes as though he had never been asleep.

"Well, my dear, shall we go now?" In the lobby he looked down at Pat and burst into laughter that rocked him almost as though he were a tall pine tree in the wind.

"Did you like the picture? I can see you did by the glow in your eyes. You may think I've wasted the afternoon by going to sleep, but I haven't. I like to go to sleep and I've made my protest against tending to business as usual. Do you understand me, miss? I've been an unregenerate old loafer and now I pronounce it officially spring."

Pat smiled at him. She didn't know what he was talking about, but she liked him and thanked him for taking her to see the picture. She still felt limp from riding that black mare.

In the entrance Jake was waiting, looking at the stills.

"She's a very charming young lady and I return her to you with reluctance. She's the goddess of spring and we've been piping it in." The judge swept her a bow with his enormous Stetson and helped her into the truck. She looked back and waved to him until they turned the corner.

"I don't know what he means all the time, do you? But he's nice."

"He always talks that way. They say he's the smartest lawyer in the state."

The truck rode more steadily going home, weighted with

bags of salt and cement. Jake was silent. He was doing arithmetic in his head, trying to work out some way of buying the electric stove and washing machine that he had seen in Rapid City. Lily would like them, but she would like the plane too. Washing machine or Piper Cub. Every time he went to town he was torn by indecision. Might as well get the plane right away and then there wouldn't be a question of these luxuries.

It was almost dark when Jake dropped Pat at her lane.

"Better come by tomorrow and see Mr. Lennox's new horses," he said. "They should be here now. His trainer's bringing three of them through in a horse van; a couple of hunters and a jumper named Lady Luck."

Pat stuck her head in the door to tell Margaret she had returned, then ran to the stable to feed Harmony. He was at the corral gate playing with Tip. As he gave her a few happy, impatient nudges, she told him about the judge and the picture show.

"Now I've seen it, honey, and I know how it's done. All we've got to do is to practice, and none of your fooling, lazybones."

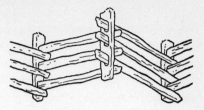

Chapter 14

The Ring

There it was, the ring marked off by a gleaming, new white board fence, and a half-dozen jumps on a flat spread of prairie at the foot of the knoll on which Mr. Lennox was building the new house. He could sit almost anywhere in his living room, look through the wall of glass and see how the horses worked. Pat noted all this as she tied Harmony to the corral fence. Mr. Lennox's plane was in front of the house, but no one was around; no one in the yard or in the kitchen, not even Ma. She went on to the stable and came upon a short, slight figure that looked like a boy, cleaning a bridle in the sun.

"Hello," said Pat tentatively.

"Hello yourself. Are you looking for Jake or somebody? They've gone to town."

"Jake said Mr. Lennox's horses would be here today."

"You're the girl that helped Jake break the colts? Yes, I brought the horses. Would you like to see them?" He got up from the box. He wasn't wearing jeans, but riding breeches and boots laced up almost to the knees. She saw that he wasn't a boy; there were too many crow's-feet around his eyes. He took her into the stable and down to the end of the long row of box

[127]

stalls. Stopping before one that housed a big, rangy bay, he patted the horse on the rump.

"Thunder, turn and let the lady see you. This is Mr. Lennox's hunter that he's ridden for a dozen years. He's getting old now and almost blind, so he's going to be turned out to loaf and have a good time. That one, War Eagle, is a hunter too. Mr. Lennox shows him in the working hunter classes and he's taken quite a few ribbons. This one," he said, pointing to a neat bay with a blaze on her face and white markings on her legs, "is Lady Luck. She's a winner. We're going to campaign with her this fall. She took a first last year at the American Royal and lots of blues at smaller shows. I shouldn't be surprised if she gets to Madison Square Garden."

Pat looked at her in awe. She was so sleek and well groomed that Pat was ashamed she hadn't begun to get rid of Harmony's rough winter hair.

The man put away the bridle and filled a water bucket. Pat looked over the collection of sponges and brushes on the shelf.

"Let me help. Have you done Thunder yet?"

The man—he said his name was Chet—gave her a slow smile. All of his movements seemed lazy, they were so quiet; but they weren't, Pat noticed. It was just that he did everything on a curve, no abrupt movements, no sharp angles.

"You can polish Lady Luck."

Chet crosstied her and War Eagle. As he picked out War Eagle's hoofs, he kept his eyes on the girl.

"You're good, kid. Lady Luck likes you. Funny how a horse knows. If you were a green hand she'd kick the stall down before she'd let you touch her."

He groomed War Eagle without giving any more attention to Pat, whistling a lonesome mountain tune as he sponged the horse's thick, black lips. The horse enjoyed it; he tried to pick up the sponge with his lips and rubbed his wet nose against Chet's sleeve.

"You going to take them over the jumps today?"

"Not this afternoon, it's too muddy; but come over in the morning and we'll try out War Eagle and Lady Luck. Thunder doesn't have to work any more. I bet a horse doesn't like to be retired any better than a man. When he sees War Eagle taking a bar, I bet he says to himself 'I could do that any day in the week and still run a fox to earth if I had to chase him all over the state of Kansas.' I wonder what Mr. Lennox'll do about hunting out here, not a wall or a rail fence in the whole country."

He was grooming War Eagle first with a brush, stroking him with the hair, making circles on his sides and rump.

"Did you ever show in any of the big shows, the American Royal or Madison Square Garden?"

Chet went to the door to tap out his currycomb.

"Sure. Lady Luck's been around and this year we're going to campaign again. Nice thing about a jumper, they don't wear out in a couple or three years like a flat racer. That's enough, kid. You've got her polished so slick I could see to shave on her."

When they had finished the grooming and put the buckets and sponges away Chet said, "That's all for today." Feeling dismissed, Pat started back to the corral. Chet came to the gate and gave her a leg up. He looked at Harmony, examined his head and ran his hands over the horse's withers.

"Good horse. A jumper or a hunter? He has the conformation. And you ride him bareback. Not many girls do that, you must be a regular cocklebur."

"Oh, I've ridden bareback ever since I was knee-high to a grasshopper."

Chet grinned. Was he making fun of her? She took Harmony toward the road at a smart pace, as fast as he could go in the mud, and looked back to see if Chet was watching her. At that moment Ty's sheep dog leaped out of a ditch after a rabbit, chasing it almost under Harmony's feet. He swerved and kicked out, sending up a shower of mud and tossing Pat into the ditch. For the moment she lay there too startled to realize what had happened; then she felt something nudge her shoulder and Harmony's cool nose against her face. She brushed the mud out of her eyes, sat up, felt her arms and legs and decided that there were no breaks, then scrambled up and glanced hastily at the corral. If Chet had seen her she could never bear to face him again. But he had gone back to the stable; there was not a soul to witness her humiliation.

There was nothing along the road from which she could mount. To be sure, she could have gone back to the corral, but her pride would not let her.

"Come on, Harmony," she said, catching the bridle, "we've got to walk home. I wish you knew how to kneel like a camel." She did not feel safe until she was over the first hump that shut off a view of the ranch.

The next morning Pat was back early to help Chet saddle War Eagle and Lady Luck and lead them to the ring. He gave her a leg up on the mare and together they cantered around the ring, limbering up the horses. Then Chet told her to keep Lady Luck out of the way while he took War Eagle over the jumps. It was all in the day's routine for War Eagle; he took the jumps with such nonchalance that they looked absurdly easy. When Chet drew up beside her Pat was sure he was going to tell her to take Lady Luck, but he didn't; he asked her to hold War Eagle while he tried out the mare.

"Couldn't I?" she asked.

"You're a good rider, kid, I've seen that, but jumping is something else again. I'm not sure you're up to it, not right off, and these are show horses. I can't take any chances with them. When I have time I'll teach you."

"But I do know how, honestly. Let me show you on Harmony."

Seeing the disappointment in her face, Chet held the bridles of War Eagle and Lady Luck while Pat ran to the corral for Harmony. Maybe she was being silly, Pat thought. Harmony might have forgotten all that he had learned last summer. It hadn't been dry enough to practice more than once or twice this spring and he never had seen these fancy jumps. Then, he had taken the three-foot rail easily after he had teased her a while and he had bucked her off playfully, just to show that he could. The lowest of these rails was three and a half feet. He never had tried one so high, but he could do it if he wanted to.

"If you don't, you lazy beggar, I'll . . . I'll put a cocklebur under your saddle. But you'd be ashamed to let me down." Harmony flicked his ear and trotted briskly into the ring.

"All right, take the low jump and then come back over it."

"Don't get tense," Pat told herself, trying to remember everything that Doc had taught her. She cantered Harmony around the ring a time or two, then put him at it, timing the take-off in rhythm with his strides, pressing her knees into the saddle and leaning forward as he rose. She was almost lying on his neck, sick in the pit of her stomach for fear he would touch. He was over, clean in front if his hind legs didn't trip the bar. He came down, light as a piece of tumbleweed and cantered off with never a buck, as though he knew this was a time to be on his good behavior. Turning him, she came back again and this time her stomach didn't contract so sharply. Harmony made it with the tiniest flick of a back hoof against the rail. Pat glanced anxiously at Chet.

"Only half a fault. He's got what it takes." Chet gave her his slow grin. "You're good too, but not so sure of yourself yet."

For over an hour they worked the horses in the bright spring sun. After she had helped Chet put the saddles on their pegs and hang up the bridles, Pat ran to the kitchen to tell Ma goodby. Ma was taking a pan of gingerbread out of the oven and smiled at Pat's quivering nose.

"You sniff just like a puppy, but you'll have to wait until it's cool enough to cut. Doc stopped by yesterday and asked if we'd seen you. Jake told him you'd been to Rapid City and made a conquest of the judge. They're old pals. Did the judge tell you he has the most famous walking horse in the Dakotas? Always gets ribbons at the American Royal."

Mr. Lennox, the judge, everybody was taking horses to the American Royal, but how would Harmony ever get there? Suddenly Pat felt defenseless, young and woefully forlorn.

"Even if Harmony is good enough to win, how am I going to get him to all these places? I haven't anything at all, not even enough to buy him a dandy brush."

Ma was accustomed to incoherent conversations; she turned a look on Pat that was almost a scowl.

"Don't ever let me hear you say that again, my girl. You've got to believe in yourself. If you believe hard enough you can do anything—anything, do you understand? And I know what I'm talking about. I haven't any time for folks who feel sorry for themselves. Now take this gingerbread and run along home. The men will be underfoot today, but they'll be scattered tomorrow. And you make good use of that Chet. Even if he does look like a runt hound pup, he knows his job."

In the morning Pat was up early to groom Harmony. She didn't have as many brushes, sponges and rubber combs as Chet, but she worked methodically, brushing the winter shagginess out of the colt's coat and oiling his hoofs, determined that he should be as smart as Lady Luck.

At Ty Chisholm's, Chet was out already with War Eagle and Lady Luck. He waved to Pat as he cantered around the ring.

"Hi, kid. Don't we look bright and shining. Bet you were up at daylight to do all that polishing. Let's put Harmony over the low bar, then we'll raise it to three foot three and nine. He ought to be able to do four before very long."

Harmony was on his good behavior; he took the bar without clowning and bucking.

"Now raise it three inches," Chet called as he brought War Eagle around from taking the coop.

Harmony was willing, but when the rail was raised to three feet three he rapped with a front foot and it came tumbling down. Harmony bolted, startled by the noise, but Pat held onto him and brought him back in a wide circle. Chet watched her with his eyes screwed up to a squint.

"Good stuff." He jumped off War Eagle and patted Harmony, quieting him and talking to him in a slow, friendly drawl. "That's all right, old fellow. Nobody expects you to do it perfectly the first time. You've schooled yourself with that knockdown. Now ride him up to it a couple of times and take him over it again. You'll get a better take-off."

Pat tried again and this time Harmony went over with plenty to spare.

"Time out," Chet called. They tied their horses to the ring fence and sat on it themselves, enjoying the sun.

"This is the kind of weather we have back home in Tennessee, only it's even nicer in the fall. My father had eight young 'uns, seven boys, and we were all the huntingest family you ever heard tell of. Horses and dogs, that's all we knew. We just couldn't bother to go to school. We didn't have any horses of our own, nothing except an old farm mule. We were as poor as Job's turkey, so we had to work with other people's horses, but we had the finest pack of hounds in the county. You ought to hear them on a clear, fall evening. Ain't no such music in the world like it."

Pat hooked her toes behind the second board and listened, following him over the hills in the moonlight, through woods the like of which she had never seen. After he had finished a cigarette, Chet put it out against the fence and gave Pat a hand down. He said she could ride Lady Luck. She took the mare over the coop, the gate and the wall, or rather, Lady Luck took Pat. The girl didn't need to think about the horse so she concentrated on her own riding, her judgment of distances and the proper moment to take off. When Chet decided that Lady Luck had worked enough he showed Pat how to teach Harmony change of pace.

"It's easy," he said. "If he's leading with his right and you're going to turn left, pull his head to the right and press with your left knee as though you were pushing his haunches to the right. When his head's pulled to the right he has to lead with the left to balance himself. Pretty soon you won't need to pull his head, he'll know what you mean when you press him with your knee. Now try it with a few figure eights."

Pat tried. It wasn't difficult to make him change lead but it was an abrupt and awkward business. They had a long way to go before Harmony did it as smoothly as Lady Luck.

It was getting late now, almost dinnertime. Jake and Mr. Lennox walked down from the barn and leaned on the ring fence.

"How you coming, honey?" Jake called.

"Want me to show you how Harmony can take the post and rail?"

Pat brought him down in front of the jump and put him at it. Maybe he was tired or not yet accustomed to the height, his front feet tucked under neatly but one of his back feet touched the rail and sent it clattering. She tried again and cleared.

"That was a good jump, cowgirl," Mr. Lennox said. "He folds nicely. He's coming along."

Chet took Lady Luck over the coop and the oxer to show Mr. Lennox her form; then he led the horses back to the stable and Pat helped him rub them down.

"If I stopped by after school could I practice Harmony a bit in the afternoons?" she asked. "He's got so much to learn, he'll never do it just on week-ends."

Chet said she could and he'd probably be around to keep an eye on her, but anyway she could use the jumps.

That night Pat went to bed early, soon after she had done the chores. She was tired and her shoulders sank gratefully against the cool horsehair mattress, but her mind would not keep still. Chet, Lady Luck and the ring had crowded so many new images, so many enticing, half-comprehended pictures into her mind that she lay staring out the window, acutely awake. It was dark outside, there was no moon; a bright star and a small one hung in the window. Presently a more substantial darkness blotted out the star. Light steps sounded and a muffled bark. Harmony had unbolted his stall door and the gate of the corral. Spring fever, he had it too. Pat slipped out of bed, ran to the window and leaned out. Harmony moved close and nibbled at her hand. Tip growled ecstatically. During the long winter the two had been inseparable. Tip had lived in Harmony's stall and played with him whenever it was warm enough to go out into the corral. When Harmony was taken out, he expected Tip to be waiting for him on his return and if the pup wasn't there he searched the barn and lot impatiently until he found his friend. Now Tip sniffed in circles around him, not going very far away.

The prairie was alive. In the daytime it was a picture to fill your eyes, but at night it had a separate existence of its own. Pat felt it moving, breathing around her. A chinook wind was blowing from the southwest, warm and restless, stirring her with impulses to strange adventures. It rustled the cheat grass and brought her the faint delicate odor of sage. It was as though she could feel the yellow bells breaking through the sod and the wild onions with their striped purple petals. Down on the creek an owl hooted plaintively. For a long time Pat stood at the window until Harmony and Tip moved on toward the creek, then, soothed, climbed into bed and went to sleep.

Chapter 15

My Incredible Baby

"How would you like to take Harmony to the county fair?" Doc called as he treated a cut on Thunder's flank. Without looking directly at Pat he watched the excitement mount in her face. "In addition to the rodeo they're going to have a very small horse show, really just an exhibition. Mr. Lennox is trying to work up an interest in jumpers and hunters in this part of the country so he's sending over War Eagle and Lady Luck, and there will be one or two other entries. It would be good training for Harmony."

Dropping the bridle she was polishing, Pat ran over to Thunder's stall.

"You know I would. Do you think we'd have a chance?"

Doc said Harmony had come along well. It was now midsummer and almost every afternoon since school closed Pat had worked him in the ring with Chet. Now he jumped four feet without concern and once or twice they had put the bars at four feet three and six.

"That's skyscraper jumping," Chet had said. "He clears with six inches of daylight under him."

Doc, watching him, had liked the way he took his jumps, standing well back like a working hunter.

It was Doc who had suggested that Harmony needed to be accustomed to a crowd. He had grown up alone and never been around people or other horses. Pat had brought over Bob and Jane and for several mornings they had done their best to act like a crowd. They borrowed pans from Ma and beat them, making a horrible clatter while Chet and Pat put the horses over the jumps. Lady Luck and War Eagle didn't flick an ear, but at first Harmony was nervous, distracted, and he had knocked down one rail after another. The carpenters who were working on the barn liked to come down and watch for a few minutes when they laid off at noon. They entered into the sport and made such a noise as the prairie had never heard. Harmony bolted, he snorted and refused, but finally when he saw that the other horses paid no attention to these unholy sounds, his pride got the better of his fear. His showmanship was so strong that he soon felt disappointed when he didn't have a shouting audience and he did better for it than when there was no one around but Pat. At these workouts alone he played, ran out and liked to buck her off, but not with an audience. The more noise they made, the better he behaved.

Training herself, Pat had been riding him bareback much of the time. Chet was as proud of her as he was of his horses. When she could take the jumps with nothing but a string about Harmony's neck, Chet assured her that she could put on a one-man show any day.

But taking the jumps with no one to watch except Chet and sometimes Doc, was one thing and riding before the crowds at a county fair, another. Already she could feel the tingling in her scalp. But the fair was a good thirty miles away. If she and Harmony could only get there!

"How could I do it, Doc?" she asked. "I'd have to ride Harmony over the day before and where would we stay all night?"

"No uncles or cousins or aunts?"

Pat shook her head.

Harmony bolted.

"Then we'll have to consult Chet and Mr. Lennox. He'll have room in the van for Harmony and I'll take you over with me. I'm going to judge the hunters and jumpers. It's to be the first week in August so you'll have three weeks to practice. Don't work Harmony too hard, you don't want him to be stale. Let him have a couple of days rest beforehand."

Giving Doc a strangling hug, Pat whirled to the corral to tell Harmony, throwing herself over the gate so full of excitement that she was like a tea kettle ready to explode if it didn't let off steam. Doc watched her tenderly. Foolish of an old man to be so concerned about a young thing's chances for happiness when nothing concerned him very deeply any more. It is only the young to whom things matter. After all, he thought with bitter wistfulness, trying to smooth their way is one of the few remaining pleasures of the old.

That afternoon when Pat ran into the kitchen she enveloped Margaret in a swift bear hug and told her about the fair. But Margaret did not respond. Pat could feel her withdrawing into herself. The girl's arms fell limp; since the close of school she had been so absorbed in the life at Ty's that she had forgotten about the old antagonisms. Indeed, Margaret had made no objections to her spending almost every day at the ranch as long as she did her chores. Now her eyes sought her mother's—big hurt eyes, Margaret saw—but she was frozen by the old dread; she could not smile or reach out and touch her daughter.

"How much is the entrance fee?" she asked drearily. This was the beginning. Now Pat would be going off just the way Sketch did and leaving her at home to dread the telephone. She couldn't stand it. She went into her room and shut the door.

Pat waited miserably outside, swallowing her tears. Presently she opened the door and found Margaret lying face down on the bed. She tiptoed over and laid her hand against her mother's face.

"Mummy, please look at me. It isn't like Sketch, honest it

isn't. There isn't any danger and you know I'd never leave
you." Margaret stirred, but she did not open her eyes. "Please,
Mummy, please, if you care so much, I won't go. I promise
you."

Margaret sat up and wiped her eyes.

"I don't want you to promise me, and I know you won't be
hurt. It's only . . . It's only . . ."

"If you don't want me to go, I won't. I won't ever go." Pat
slipped her hand over Margaret's. The cold fingers stirred and
curled under hers.

"I'm not really a selfish prig." Margaret got up and smoothed
her hair. "Come out in the kitchen now and tell me all about it."

Having made up her mind to let Pat go to the fair, Margaret
undertook to find out the practical details. She called up Doc
and asked him about the entrance fee and what Pat was supposed to wear. He said he had wanted to see her and would
stop by the following afternoon while Pat was at Ty's.

"My dear, you are always a joy to the eye," he greeted Margaret with appreciation of the cool fresh print and the smooth
brow under the coronet.

"You always make me feel at my best, Doc. I couldn't be too
selfish or unreasonable when I'm with you. Will you have your
coffee hot or cold? I haven't ice, but there is a bottle of it in the
well."

As they sat in the cool log kitchen protected from the dust
and the blistering heat of the July afternoon, Doc and Margaret
found comfort in each other. He told her about Mr. Lennox
persuading the fair committee to put on a horse show in addition to the rodeo, walking horses and jumping, not much of a
show for there wouldn't be more than a couple of thoroughbred exhibitors. He would have room for Harmony in Chet's
van. The entrance fee was three dollars. Pat said she had saved
that much egg money.

"What about clothes? Can she ride in jeans?"

"Margaret, if you'll let me, and I hope you will for I'm an old man and there aren't very many things I want to do, I'd like to give her a riding habit." Margaret flushed. Doc put his hand on hers across the table as though to hush her.

"Don't say it. I know all the protests you'd like to make, but balance against them the pleasure it would give me and the sense of fulfillment for her. It was the one thing Sketch promised her and it has a special value for her. You don't really mind when you think of it this way."

Margaret sighed.

"You're right, of course. You always are. To oppose you would be to make me more inflexible and ungracious than I am. But, Doc, remember she's my baby—all I have. You won't let this thing take her away from me?"

So it was arranged. Jake's new plane had come and he was taking Doc to Kansas City one day soon. Margaret gave him Pat's measurements and the size of her shoes.

"Let's not tell her," he suggested, "until I bring them. I'd like to watch her face."

Happy that Margaret no longer opposed her, Pat flung herself into schooling Harmony. She got up at five o'clock, gobbled a cold breakfast, groomed Harmony and reached the ring a little after six. Usually Chet was there with Lady Luck and War Eagle. The horses felt good in the early morning when the air was fresh, before the sun came out and a hot wind blew dust in their faces. Sometimes Bob rode over to see how they were doing. He was entered in the rodeo and he was going to show Cindy as a cutting horse.

The day Doc came home from Kansas City, Jake dropped him at Margaret's. It was almost dark and Pat had just come from Ty's. She was in the barn doing Harmony for the night. When she came in Doc and Margaret were at the supper table.

"Wash yourself extra well," Margaret said, "and go in and look on your bed."

When she had scrubbed her face and hands, Pat darted into the bedroom. Margaret and Doc waited, smiling at each other. Pat took a long time. At last she came to the door and stood there in a trance.

"Doc! Mummy!" Her voice quivered with awe.

"Don't be so solemn about it. Go and put them on. We want to see if they fit. Smile, monkey face."

Pat flung herself on Doc with a mighty hug, then went into her room and slammed the door.

"Too much emotion, too much everything," sighed Margaret, but she couldn't resist a smile tinged with irony as she watched Doc smooth his hair and straighten the neck of his coat.

In a few moments Pat returned shyly in sand-colored whip-cord riding breeches, a black coat, a high white stock and a yellow vest, the cap perched too far back on her head.

"Stand up," said Margaret. "Don't slouch. Come over and let's see how it fits."

Doc squinted his eyes as though he were looking at a sick horse.

"Do you know, she's almost grown. I didn't realize it. The fit is very good. Put the cap forward the way I told you. The visor is supposed to keep the sun out of your eyes. Now take off the coat and see how the shirt looks. You won't need to wear the vest at the fair." In the tailored white shirt and breeches she looked even taller, more grown-up.

"You'll do, monkey. Do you think you can get around in the boots? They'll seem awkward at first. You'd better ride in them this week," Doc said, smiling.

After the first awe of the habit wore off, Pat was so enchanted with it that she made excuses every few minutes to go into her room and look in the mirror. When Jake came to pick Doc up she strutted before him, clicking her heels and flicking her crop against the chairs.

"Some peacock, eh, Doc. Be too bad if Harmony bucks you off in those fine feathers."

The afternoon before the show Pat rode Harmony over to Ty's and walked back. Chet was going to start off by six or seven in the morning so he'd have plenty of time to braid and groom the horses. As Doc was to pick up Pat at about seven-thirty they wouldn't be much later. Soon after daylight Pat fed the chickens and brought in the water. Long before Doc came she was dressed in the new habit, all but the boots which stood ready by the door. When Doc tooted she threw her arms around Margaret's neck.

"Good-by, Mommy. Wish me luck." She ran to the car carrying the boots. Margaret waved them out of sight then she walked quietly to her mother's rocking chair and sank into it, resting her hands on its arms. She closed her eyes; she was tired, very tired and shaken with fears. She was lonely and shut out. Memories of her childhood in this very room crowded about her, faint, happy ghosts of the time when she was safe, and when the world revolved around her. But Sketch had changed all that. He was the sun and she the satellite. She could never break away from his attraction—or want to—but once, just once, she would like to be the most important thing in someone's life.

The jingling of the telephone bell snapped her back to reality. Two longs, one short, her ring, Ma probably, wanting to gossip about the fair. She felt in no mood for chatter, but it might be something important. She took down the receiver. A man's voice that she didn't recognize asked, "Mrs. Cole?" It was Mr. Lennox; he, Jake and Ty were flying over to the fair and had room for her if she would like to go. They would be at home by dark as Jake had to look after the stock.

Margaret's heart missed a beat, halted by indecision. She

wanted to be near her baby in her big moment, but if there
should be an accident, if Pat should break a leg or an arm,
wouldn't it be much worse to actually see it happen? No, even
at the very worst her imagination could conjure, she wanted
to be there with her little girl instead of waiting alone at home
as she had done so many times. Her emotions in a turmoil, but
her voice cool, she answered, "Yes, thank you, I should like
very much to go." Why she had said "yes" so glibly, she could
not explain. Now she began to worry for fear she had done the
wrong thing. How would Pat like her being there? Would it
make her more nervous? Pat need not know until her event was
over.

Doc drove into the fair grounds through the back entrance
reserved for exhibitors. As he went to the office for their passes
Pat caught a glimpse of the midway, the ferris wheel and
merry-go-round, the booths empty so early in the morning,
still littered with candy wrappings and empty popcorn bags.
But she scarcely saw them nor heard the sheep, chickens, pigs,
cattle, grunting, squeaking, cackling, she was so jittery inside.
If she could just get to Harmony, see that he was all right, and
ride him around a bit to limber him up, she would get back her
confidence.

The stalls were alive with excitement, stableboys grooming
cow ponies, paints, apaloosas, combing the tails of palominos,
owners comparing notes, officials milling around. Pat saw the
Lennox stalls first, gave Chet an excited "Hi," and was out of
the car before Doc had time to brake. He smiled at her eagerness, handed her boots to Chet and drove away without waiting
for another word with her. She had made for Harmony's stall
and was going over him inch by inch.

Chet gave her his slow smile. The grooming was done, all
three of the horses gleamed like satin, but the tack had to be
sorted and gone over to remove the dust of the road. Lady Luck's

mane already was braided and Chet was starting on War Eagle; he offered to do Harmony, too, but Pat believed that if she did it herself it would bring her luck. A few days earlier Chet had pulled Harmony's mane to the right length and thinned it. Pat divided it with her eye into seven sections and began on the first pigtail. Every now and then when she thought she was doing a good job on the stubborn mane she looked at Lady Luck's neatly braided neck and took out what she had done to begin again. At last she finished and stood back to admire the braids. Harmony seemed to understand that these little plaits bobbing on his neck were intended to enhance his beauty so he tossed his head proudly to show them off.

"Time out for lunch," Chet decided. He said he would braid their tails after lunch and Pat could look at the amusements.

She was surprised that it was twelve o'clock; the very thought of food made butterflies dance in her stomach.

"I don't believe I want anything. Honest, I just couldn't."

"All right, kid, I know how you feel. I won't be long."

While Chet was gone Pat dusted her boots and set them in front of the stall. In less than fifteen minutes he returned with a hamburger and a bottle of milk.

"Down this, kid," he insisted. "You're going to need it."

Pat thought she could never swallow the milk, but strangely it felt cool and soothing. Chet bridled Harmony and suggested that Pat take him out and find a patch of grass for him to nibble. He was excited too and that would calm him down. Then she should give him a look at the show ring and the crowd. She jumped on him bareback and rode outside the ring, letting him nibble, telling him how important it was that they do well at their first show.

"Even if you don't win, old darling, you'll make a good showing. I'm going to be terribly proud of you."

Not far from the ring Pat noticed a little picket fence and her heart which had settled to a steady beat began to race again.

After trotting Harmony a bit she headed him toward the fence. It wasn't high enough to worry him, but he didn't like the look of it and ran out.

"Oh, Harm," she patted his neck, "it was my fault. I was too excited, not positive enough. Come on, we'll try it again." This time Harmony responded to her confidence and went over without a moment's hesitation.

Noticing a man mounted on a beautiful gray with an English saddle, Pat suddenly remembered that it must be almost time for her class and she had not put on her boots. Jumping off Harmony she led him on a brisk trot to the stable. Chet was waiting for her, the horses all tacked up.

"Easy now, not so much excitement. Slow down, you're red as a beet. Our class has just been called. Here, give me the horse while you put on your boots. Doc came by to wish you luck."

Chet gave Pat a leg up and she followed him to the paddock. She looked nervously at the other horses, anxiously noting their obvious good points. There were only two others, the gray hunter she had seen outside the ring and a beautiful young chestnut mare who was shy and skittish. She didn't like the noise and jumped as the rodeo crowds cheered, laying back her ears and rolling her eyes.

Pat's number was five. As the jumps were set up in the ring she took Harmony outside, trotting and cantering a little. The jumps weren't too hard, six of them, all three feet nine, to be raised for a jump-off in case of a tie; but to Pat in her nervousness they looked at least six feet. She saw Doc standing in the middle of the ring, very smart in jodhpurs and gleaming boots.

Lady Luck was first in the ring, and Pat, watching the ease with which she skimmed over the course, whispered to Harmony, "That's the horse to beat." The first time around Lady Luck took the jumps without a fault, but on the second go her hind foot touched the post and rail. Chet was annoyed when he brought her back, saying she should have cleared that easily, it was only three feet nine.

The gray didn't do so well; one front tick and one knockdown. War Eagle disgraced himself with two knockdowns. The mare was so jittery that Chet said she would never get around the course, but when she took the first jump he opened his eyes.

"Gosh! she's jumping over the moon. Wish I could get my hands on her."

But he was right, she refused to take the wall and danced all over the field in such a state of nerves that after three refusals she was ruled out.

"What she needs is a good rider. That lad isn't positive enough," Chet pointed out. Remembering the picket fence Pat shivered, but she believed in Harmony, he wouldn't quit.

"Number five." It was Pat's turn. Chet gave Harmony's rump a pat.

"Go on in, kid and show them what you can do."

Gathering up the reins Pat settled herself in the saddle, leaned down and whispered to Harmony, "Come on, my pet, we can do it." As she rode into the ring she tried to remember all the things Doc had told her. "First make a wide circle," she checked off in her mind, "let Harmony take a look at the nearest jumps and on the turn begin to trot, swinging into a collected canter."

Everything was happening so fast that she only half heard the cheers of the crowd, it was as though she were moving in a sort of vacuum. Harmony was as composed as a veteran actor taking a curtain call. He cleared one jump after another with gusto, no knockdown, no tick. She was beginning to breathe naturally. The second go around was just as good until the very last jump, the gate, which he ticked with his hind foot.

As she rode out of the ring Pat leaped to the ground before

Harmony had entirely stopped and kissed his star, letting him rub his head against her new coat. Half pushed, half leading him, she reached the entrance gate. She wasn't sure, but she thought he had won a second. And in his first show!

Chet took Harmony's reins.

"You were magnificent, kid. We're rivals now, you and Lady Luck. They'll probably raise the rail to four feet but you can do it. Yes, there they go." He jumped on Lady Luck, as his number was called. Pat was so out of breath that she couldn't look. When he came back she was still leaning against Harmony, mopping the wet curls under her cap.

"Jumped clean as a whistle," Chet answered the question in her eyes. He gave her a leg up.

"You can do it."

This time as she rode out, Pat's heart was not pounding so hard. "Even if he misses now, Harmony will get a second," she thought. "He has proved himself." She settled lightly in the saddle, prepared to give the order at the exact moment. Harmony lifted smoothly and came down clean, in a great arc that scarcely jolted her as he picked up his canter.

When she returned to the paddock Chet was already up.

"Four feet three this time. Aren't you nervous?" He was already at the gate when his number was called. Pat sat on Harmony and watched. Lady Luck took jump after jump seemingly effortlessly. She had just one jump left for another clean performance. It was a beautiful take-off, her front feet cleared, she was coming down, she was making it—no, she touched. Half a fault. Harmony could never beat that. Chet brought Lady Luck back out of the ring, ducking her head as she always did when she made a fault.

"Good luck," he called.

The crowd gave Pat a great cheer as she and Harmony came through the gate. She glanced at Doc, but he stood near the center of the ring, very dignified and official, not even a smile.

Pat couldn't watch, but she wondered if he would give the little unconscious kick with which he always helped Harmony over the jumps.

"Well, here we go," she whispered to Harmony. "Can you do it, pet?"

The louder the crowd roared the more confidently Harmony moved down the course. Pat relaxed; she was with him on every jump, talking to him, telling him he could do it. Even when he got in wrong for the take-off on the seventh jump, he miraculously twisted himself over it without touching. He finished the course without a fault.

In the confusion that followed, Pat was smothered in a crowd of people who wanted to shake her hand. Doc was giving her the trophy, a handsome silver platter, and pinning a blue ribbon on Harmony's bridle. Now he was smiling as though she were the apple of his eye. The judge, who stood out above the others like a skyscraper on a prairie, invited her to have a hot fudge sundae. Somebody was calling to her to hold Harmony's bridle and look into the camera. She put her arm around the horse and rubbed her hot face against his neck.

Mr. Lennox put his hand on her shoulder and swung her around to face Margaret. Her mother was smiling and her lashes were wet.

"Mummy, you saw us! Did we do all right? Are you proud of us?"

Margaret dabbed at Pat's flushed damp face with her handkerchief.

"Of course, I'm proud. My baby, my own incredible baby."

Chapter 16

The Barn Dance

The barn was done, its wood a little paler than the gold of the August prairie. Mr. Lennox invited the neighbors to a house-warming. On the day of the party, Ma circled around the kitchen like a bumblebee, making sandwiches. Margaret had baked three cakes, and Pat helped with the icing. It was so hot that Margaret did not need to heat water for their baths, Pat had filled the tub by the kitchen door and the water was still lukewarm from the sun.

"Scrub yourself well with kitchen soap to get rid of the stable smell and then I'll give you some of my toilet water."

As she splashed in the tub, Pat watched Margaret dress. The chest of drawers in her mother's room was directly opposite the open door. Before the old shaving mirror tilted on its two posts, Margaret brushed her hair. Following the rhythmic sweep of the brush over the ripples that the plaits had left gave Pat pleasure. She liked the graceful arch of Margaret's raised arms as she rewound the plaits and stuck into the coronet the garnet star that had belonged to her mother. To the closet and back, Margaret disappeared and came again into the picture, framed by the door. Sitting in the old swan rocker she thrust her feet into her party slippers, white suede pumps that she had worn the summer she married Sketch. The toes were a little too pointed now, but they were still good. Over her head she slipped her new dress, the pale blue dotted swiss that she had made from material for which she had traded eggs in Sorum. The full skirt billowed around her like the petals of a morning glory.

"Mummy darling," Pat gasped as she wiped soap from her eyes, "you're as beautiful as Empress Eugenie in our history. I wish you could always stay dressed up."

Margaret blushed, but she looked pleased.

"Hurry now, don't talk such nonsense, sweet."

Pat dried herself and looked in the kitchen mirror at a face so shiny that you would have thought it had been scrubbed with silver polish. On her bed lay her own new dress, a pink dotted swiss with tiny puffed sleeves and a ruffle around the neck. When she put it on she felt self-conscious as though her neck and arms were beanstalks.

At eight o'clock the prairie was only half hidden in the soft blue twilight; the Ford roared through the stillness like a snorting dragon. In the new barn, Jake had made seats along the walls with planks laid on boxes and at one end a trestle table on which Margaret and Ma arranged the cakes and sandwiches, covering them with a gay, red-checked tablecloth. Mr. Lennox came out to help. Cars began to park behind the barn, Ed Lancaster, Bob and Jane, the Yateses with their new baby that they laid on one end of the table on a pillow, Jake, and Lily, the yellow-haired teacher of the little school in the buttes, all the neighbors for thirty miles around. Mr. Lennox sprinkled wax on the floor and while they waited for the dancing to start, the children skated on it. Pat listened with one ear as she and Bob climbed the ladder to investigate the loft.

"That horse of Pat's has the makings of a champion. And beautifully trained. Thanks, no doubt, to Doc." Mr. Lennox was talking to Margaret.

"Don't forget, Chet had a hand in it." Doc stroked his moustache as he always did when he was pleased. "And, while we're passing out the orchids, he couldn't have been better ridden."

Mr. Lennox was resting his eyes approvingly on Margaret's coronet.

"What are you going to do with your young horsewoman? She's not going to hide her light under a bushel."

Pat didn't hear the answer, but she saw Margaret flush and thought again how radiant her mother was when her eyes lighted up. Bob was looking out the loft door. Pat helped him try the winch for pulling up hay. He offered to swing her down on the hook, but she was afraid to tear her dress. She did snag it coming down the ladder, but Bob said it didn't show.

Presently the music came, a rancher from over Sorum way; a thin-faced, frail-looking widower who brought along his two children. He played the accordion for local dances and when the children were sleepy they went to bed on a couple of pillows on the floor. Jake brought a chair and set it in the corner opposite the table. The rancher ran his hands over the keys to limber his fingers and call in the men who were talking in groups outside in the dark.

Doc came over to Pat.

"May I have this one? It's going to be a waltz. I'm a little too old for the acrobatics of the butterfly."

Pat liked to dance with Doc even though he was deliberate and formal. He had danced with her ever since she was tall enough to reach up to his waist. So had all of Sketch's friends. She couldn't remember when she had learned to dance, it had been as natural as learning to ride. All children came to the dances, mothers danced with their five- or six-year-old sons, miniature Hopalong Cassidy's in cowboy boots and dangling wooden pistols, and fathers guided their little daughters around the floor.

"I'm so proud of you I could crow." Doc swung Pat out of the way of an old cowboy, who was cutting extra capers with his heels. "But you mustn't let up. One way or another we're going to get to some of the big shows this fall and you want to be in top form."

"We'll get to work again tomorrow, and I'll put up another five-foot rail. Did I bring him down right? How was my hold on the reins?"

The music stopped; the accordion player wiped his forehead and looked over his shoulder to see how his son was behaving. The two-year-old was sitting on his pillow peeping gravely between the legs of his father's chair.

Doc and Pat looked for Margaret and found her with Ma, Ty and Mr. Lennox, all of them laughing. Ma was fanning herself vigorously.

"Land's sake, Mr. Lennox, you knocked the breath right out of me. I'm no young filly. How do you expect me at my age to gyrate like a windmill in a blow?"

"That from the girl I couldn't keep in shoes, she danced them out so fast!" Ty clapped Ma on the back with his mighty paw and she punched him with her fan. As the music started, Mr. Lennox took Margaret's hand. Doc grinned wickedly at Ma.

"Well, old cart horse." They were off on one of their bouts of joyful insults.

Pat saw Eric Schwartz solemnly practicing in a corner, one arm around an imaginary partner and the other held up in the air.

"Come on, cowboy and give me a whirl." Pat took him out onto the floor and was surprised that he was able to keep in step. Mr. Lennox danced with her, and Ed Lancaster and Bob, although Bob said he'd rather stay outside and listen to the men.

Pat looked around for Chet, but did not see him until almost time for supper. In ordinary clothes he looked more than ever like an undersized boy. He came over to the table where she had been sneaking a sandwich from under the red tablecloth.

"Watch out," she warned him, "you're leaning on the baby."

He jumped back as though a snake had hissed at him.

"My Lord, a baby here! They keep them at home where I come from. And this one's sleeping as sound as though his mammy was rocking him in a cradle! Wouldn't you think he'd be yowling with all this noise? They must set off firecrackers at his head every evening to keep him in training."

The accordionist began a lonesome tune that Chet whistled as he put his arm around Pat. He danced well, loosely and smoothly. When the music stopped he took her to the door and they stepped out into the cool evening. He walked to the corner of the barn and glanced around to see that he wasn't overheard. "I've news for you," he said. "Maybe I oughtn't to tell you, but I thought you'd like to know before it was sprung on you. Mr. Lennox is going to make you an offer for Harmony. Five thousand dollars. That's a pile for a horse that's only shown once, but the boss is a good sort. He figures five thousand will pretty well set you up and do the things your ranch needs. He's a great admirer of your mother and thinks she's awfully plucky to carry on alone the way she does." *

Sell Harmony! Pat took hold of Chet's arm; her fingers dug into his sleeve. For a minute she could not comprehend what he had said. Her stomach contracted into a lump and she was afraid she was going to be sick.

"Now, kid, don't let it get you."

"I'm not. It's just that I can't quite take it in. What in the world would I do without Harmony?"

"Get yourself another colt and train him. Mr. Lennox will let you have a good one cheap and I'll help you with him. Don't ever let yourself get to thinking there's only one horse in the world. It doesn't do. I felt that way once about a little mule. She was the prettiest pacer this side of heaven, and I was working on her the way I had seen the trainers at the stables where I carried water and walked the colts. I was only nine years old, but I knew a lot about horses. That mule had five gaits and was the smoothest thing on hoofs. One day after I had been showing her off to the man who owned the farm next door, he offered seventy-five dollars for her, and Pa sold her. I went out to the barn and dug into the straw and nearly yowled my eyes out. But there were others. You don't think there'll ever be another for you now, but there will be."

Chet was talking at random to give Pat a chance to get hold of herself. He hated to do this to her, but he figured it would be better for her to have some time to think about the idea.

"If you love horses you've got a heart big enough for more than one, Pat. You can be sure of that. Anyway, you don't have to sell Harmony unless you want to. That's the reason I told you." He whistled a bar or two of the lonesome tune. "Some night, isn't it? Look at the Little Dipper up there, so bright you could take it out and put it in your hair and folks 'ud think you're wearing diamonds."

Pat looked up automatically. She refused to believe what Chet had told her. She couldn't—but the enormity of it was still twisting in her like a knife. She wanted to double up, as though she were in pain, but she stood stock still and looked at the Little Dipper until her breath stopped hurting. It seemed to be leering at her.

Chet caught her hand. He ran to the door, drawing her after him.

"There's the butterfly. Come on, let's take a whirl."

A languorous tune drifted out to them, four slow hesitating bars followed by a quartet of frenzied ones that set the blood pounding. For the butterfly one needed a third. Bob was edging toward them, skirting the dancers. They put their arms around Pat's waist, one on each side. To the dragging tempo they promenaded, holding a step with the toe pointed for an entire bar, then to the mad acceleration Pat swung them alternately. Dancers shrieked as they bounced into each other and hooked arms for another fling.

Then another languid interlude. Pat swung and pointed, swung and pointed. She still locked what Chet had told her out of her mind, but it was right behind her shoulder, ready to crawl in the minute it had a chance. She wouldn't let it—not now, not until she could be alone where no one could see her.

It was a good party. Toward eleven o'clock after the men had made several trips to the old barn where Mr. Lennox had cached a good supply of whiskey—it was not polite to serve liquor at mixed parties, and the men enjoyed swigging their drinks from a bottle—Ma brought from the house an enormous battered coffeepot, relic of many picnics. Everybody crowded around the table; the children waked up; the dancers sat in little groups on the benches or the floor, laughing and shrieking as they balanced their paper cups. The accordionist came out of his corner and drank a cupful at a gulp before he bit into a sandwich.

After supper the dancing was wilder, more butterflies and square dances, more swinging and tittering. By midnight the guests with young children said good night. Margaret thought it time to go home, but Mr. Lennox asked her to wait. He didn't want her to drive alone and as soon as the party was over he would take her. Pat wanted to go; she had to do something about the tension inside her head. She and Bob practiced the conga until the Lancasters went home, then, as the guests thinned out, she helped Ma collect paper cups and plates. Finally the accordionist carried his sleepy children to the car, taking along half a cake that Ma wrapped up for him. Mr. Lennox saw off the last of his guests, then brought the blue convertible out of the barn. The three of them sat in front, Pat stared at the fan of the headlights and shivered in the cool night breeze that the speed of the car whipped up. She did not hear the words the others said, she wanted to get home, to shut the door of her room, to be alone. Nothing but tears would loosen this clamp in her head.

After supper the dancing was wilder.

They crossed the little culvert where Margaret's lane met the road. Mr. Lennox stopped before the kitchen door. He helped them out and said something about bringing the Ford over tomorrow afternoon. They bade each other good night. In the kitchen Margaret sank into her rocker beside the table and kicked off her shoes.

"Would you like a glass of milk?" she asked Pat. She wanted to talk about the party. It was not very kind to leave her when she was still alight with the excitement of the dance and eager to discuss the news that she had gathered from Ma, the Lancasters and the schoolteacher with the yellow hair, but Pat could not listen. If she didn't get away by herself she was afraid she would burst out crying. But she kept her voice steady as she answered, "No, thank you, Mummy, I just think I'll go to bed."

"All right, honey." Margaret got up in her stocking feet and locked the kitchen door.

In her own room Pat stepped from her clothes and put out the light. She threw herself face down on the bed, but the tightness would not go. If only she could cry someplace where no one would hear her. Climbing out the window she ran across the yard, climbed over the corral gate and felt her way into the pitch black stable. Tip came out to her with little welcoming yaps. Harmony twitched an ear, but gave no other sign that he was awake. She sat on an upturned bucket in the corner of the stall. Tip crawled into her lap. Her misery swept over her like a flood. In her desperate loneliness she wanted her father.

"Sketch," she whispered, "where are you? I need you." She sat motionless, waiting to feel him beside her, to hear him laughing and calling to her, "I'm here, Patsy Pie." She held her breath and put her hand over Tip's nose to keep him quiet. Tiny night noises creaked and rustled in the barn, a swallow stirred in its nest, a rat crept down from the loft, but Sketch did not come. Yet, little by little, the tension eased. Now that she could cry, the need was gone. There was no struggle. She knew that she would sell Harmony. Every time she thought of Margaret, flushed and beautiful, looking at Mr. Lennox with starry eyes, she knew she had no choice. How could she selfishly keep Harmony when she had it in her power to give Margaret a bathroom, bottled gas, pretty things for the house, new dresses? You just couldn't refuse to give another person what she wants, not when you love her. And Pat loved Margaret with a double love, one for herself and one for Sketch. She was a part of him, the only part that was left, and she could make up to Margaret for the things he might have given her. Maybe he never would have, but it was like being able to pay off a debt hanging over your beloved. It sets him free.

What would she do without Harmony? She didn't want to think about that. Now it would be like the terrible first summer after Sketch's death before she had Harmony to love.

"But Chet's wrong," she said, too low to awaken Harmony. "Don't think there ever will be another horse like you. I just couldn't set my heart on another one." Tip rolled over and licked her hand.

Chapter 17

Panache

Mr. Lennox came the next morning while Pat was grooming Harmony. Pat didn't go to the house. Even though her mind was made up and she knew nothing could save Harmony for her, she dreaded hearing the actual words. So she sponged his mane and tail and picked out his hoofs, trying to say to him by her ministrations, "Please don't forget me. No one else will ever love you the way I do."

Presently Margaret came to the kitchen door and called. Pat squeezed the sponge and threw out the water, she didn't bother to smooth back her hair or dust her jeans. Margaret was wearing her old rose and white striped dress but it was freshly ironed and made her look as delicious as a stick of peppermint candy. She and Mr. Lennox had been having coffee, the wedding ring pot was on the table and what was left of the chocolate cake. Margaret had gathered a handful of purple thistles that stood in a blue glass jug.

"Pat," she said, "Mr. Lennox has a matter of business to talk over with you. It is entirely your affair. Whatever you decide, you mustn't consider me one way or another. I expect he'd rather tell you by yourself, so I'll go out to the barn and look for eggs."

Pat couldn't help smiling although her heart was constricted like a squeezed lemon. What a fibber her mother was; in that fresh dress she would go nowhere near the barn. When she had crossed the door, Pat steeled herself to keep her face composed, she didn't want anyone in the world to know how bad she felt.

"I've just been talking with your mother about Harmony. You have a great horse, Pat, and I believe if he's given the proper chance he has the makings of a champion. It isn't every horse that can beat Lady Luck the first time he meets her, for she's almost as good as they come. You know she has won a fistful of blue ribbons in the big shows and I'm counting on her to win more this fall. I'd like to take Harmony when we start out in a couple of weeks. If he shows up as well as I think he will, we'll enter him at the American Royal. Would you sell him to me? I told your mother I'd give you five thousand for him."

Pat tried to keep her mouth from quivering. She knew she must answer quickly before she changed her mind.

"Yes, I . . . I want him to have his chance in the American Royal. You can take him."

Mr. Lennox laid his hand on her shoulder, surprised and relieved that she should have consented so easily.

"Good girl," he said. "Then that's all settled. Bring him over to Chet tomorrow; he'll be glad to have you help him with the workouts if you want to. You know Chet will be good to him." Mr. Lennox took his checkbook from his pocket and laid it on the table. "Shall I make it out to you or your mother?"

"Mother, please. I haven't a bank account."

Mr. Lennox tore out the check and laid it on the table.

"What are you going to do with it, make things a little more convenient for your mother I hope, and use some of it for high school next year. You are going on to school, aren't you, Pat? You're a bright girl and should go to college. And Pat," he hesitated as though there were something else he wanted to say, then thought better of it and offered her his hand. "We're neighbors, you know, and you can always call on me. You'd tell me, wouldn't you, if your mother ever gets into difficulties? She's carrying too much for a woman."

Pat's hand lay limp in his. It was so cold that he wondered if she were having a chill.

"You all right?" he asked anxiously.

"Yes, it's just that I can't get used to things so quickly. I guess there's a lot I can do for Mother."

"That's the girl." Mr. Lennox laid a friendly hand on her shoulder. When he went out to the blue convertible, Margaret came from the soddy to see him off.

"I'll be over before I leave," he said, "and this winter I'm going to be around a lot."

Pat gave Margaret the check and she looked at it curiously; she never had seen so much money at one time. Neither she nor Pat mentioned Harmony. Later that night when Pat went to bed, Margaret put an arm around her and kissed her.

"You didn't need to do it, dear. You know that, don't you?"

"Yes, Mummy, but I wanted to. Don't you remember the things I told you I was going to do?" She ran into her room and closed the door.

The next afternoon Pat rode Harmony bareback over to Ty's. Mr. Lennox wasn't there, but she left the colt with Chet in the stable; she didn't feel sure enough of herself to see Jake or Ma.

Chet didn't say anything, he couldn't find the right word, so he led Harmony to a stall that had been cleaned out and brought a fresh bucket of water.

"You honestly do think he has a chance, don't you?"

"Yes, I do, and you know I'll take good care of him."

"There's just one thing. Do you think you could take Tip along? They've never been separated and Harmony gets awfully cross and nervous when he doesn't find Tip in the stall. He doesn't go to sleep without the pup."

Chet scratched his head.

"I just don't see how it can be done. We'll be traveling by van and it's going to be awfully crowded with three horses and me in it. I even have to leave my hound behind. Mr. Lennox doesn't want him to clutter up the van, and I'm afraid he would feel the same way about Tip. But when we come back for the winter, you can bring him over. How will that do?"

Pat sighed as she unfastened the bridle and drew it over Harmony's head. She didn't tell him good-by, not in front of Chet.

"You'll come over and help me work him before we go? If you'll wait until Jake comes back with the carryall, I'll drive you home."

"Never mind. It isn't much of a walk." Throwing the bridle over her shoulder, she walked down the lane without looking back. Chet watched her with a worried pucker on his face.

"She's all broken up, poor kid. She thinks this is the end and she never wants to see the horse or any one of us again."

With Harmony gone there was nothing to do, no reason for going to the stable or the meadow. Nor could Pat endure the house. Margaret was particularly gentle, sensing Pat's loneliness, but she could not hide her own relief. She tried to interest Pat in plans for spending the money. If they were going to put in a bathroom, it should be done right away. They would probably need to get a contractor from Rapid City. And Pat would need clothes for the winter if she was going to Bison. Wouldn't she like to go to Rapid City and shop?

Yes, of course, there was no reason why she shouldn't go, but every suggestion that her mother made sharpened the hurt, and Pat was ashamed that it should be so. She had sold Harmony of her own free will and she wanted to do these things for her mother, but secretly she felt outraged that Margaret should be so happy about them.

She hadn't gone back to see Ty and Ma and would not go until Chet had taken Harmony away. And she had not seen

Doc. One afternoon when she and Tip were lying in the shade of the willows by the creek, she saw Doc's pickup coming along the road. Her first impulse was to sit still; she didn't want him to ask about Harmony, but she was so lonely and unhappy that she had to talk to someone. She crawled out of the willows into the sun, stood up and waved to him. He turned the car from the road into the prairie.

"I was coming to your house," he said. "Get in, Tip too if he wants."

Gathering up Tip, she climbed in beside him. Doc slammed the door and continued toward the Lancasters'. For a while neither of them said a word.

"Well," Doc demanded finally, "why in the world did you do it? You didn't have to. You know we were going to get Harmony to the horse shows one way or another."

"Yes, but I didn't really have any choice. Think of all the things that money's going to do for Mummy. I couldn't be a selfish pig, could I?"

Doc grunted.

"No, I suppose you couldn't, but sometimes unselfishness is a vice. You've got to be yourself. You've got to fight for your own integrity as a person. Sketch knew it, that's what made him Sketch. But, poor kid, you're not old enough and tough enough. And I'm talking nonsense. You did a magnificent thing, honey."

Pat burst into tears.

"Go on, have a good cry. I expect you've been holding in all this time. Sorry I can't wipe your eyes, got to look for badger holes. There's a clean hanky in my vest pocket."

The girl fumbled for it and dabbed her eyes. Presently she spread it out on her knees.

"There, I feel better. Where are we going, to see one of Mr. Lancaster's cows?"

It wasn't a cow, but a horse—Ed Lancaster's pickup horse.

He had a fistula, a boil on his withers, very painful, Doc told her. Doc had to lance the abscess and cut away the infected tissue around it. When they reached the Lancaster stable, Pat helped Doc sterilize his hands and gave him his scalpels; she filled his syringe with disinfectant and watched him clean out the hole, apply sulfa ointment and grease the hide around it with Vaseline to protect the hair. Bob, who held the horse's head, was impressed; he listened carefully as Doc told him how to keep the wound open and prevent the flies from bothering it. Bob hadn't heard about Harmony; he was still talking about his calf-roping prize.

On the way back Doc left the road again and cut across the prairie, twisting to avoid clumps of white and purple asters and yellow sedum.

"If it weren't so hot," he said, mopping his damp forehead, "this would be the loveliest time of the year." He looked over the meadows where the pink flowering tumbleweed and thistles and once in a while yellow patches of dragonhead and sorrel made the pasture seem like a flowered carpet. Pat got out and picked an armful of asters, even though she knew they wouldn't last long. Doc glanced at her gray face with the light blotted out and cudgeled his brain.

"Good girl," he said, sticking an aster in his buttonhole. "Now let's forget our troubles. What are we going to do for the rest of the summer? We mustn't waste these next two golden months. Would you like to be my assistant lady vet until you go to school? We could jaunt all over these parts and do a lot of exploring. You already know a good deal about doctoring and you could really help me."

"Oh, Doc, could I!" Pat threw her arms around Doc's neck, sending the pickup careening across the track. "I've been so lonely I could hardly stand it. Will you stop for me tomorrow? Will you?"

He gave her a teasing smile, marveling how her spirits had

bounced from low to high. As he let her out at her own lane he promised to fix up a little medicine kit for her.

Now that Harmony was gone, Tip had attached himself to Pat and never left her heels. He woofed excitedly at Mr. Lennox's car parked before the back door. Its owner and Margaret were in the kitchen, but Pat did not stay with them very long for they were talking grown-up talk that shut her out; she and Tip went to dust her gear in the soddy.

Almost every day Mr. Lennox came over. He offered Pat his carpenters for a few days to put up a lean-to for the bathroom and advised her about what sort of liquid gas to use and the best kind of heater for the hot water. He probably had talked it all over with Margaret too, but was careful to emphasize before Pat that the decisions were hers.

The carpenters were old friends of Pat's. Helping Margaret cook for them on days when she wasn't out with Doc kept Pat so busy that she was too tired at night to stare out the window at the corrals and eat out her heart for Harmony.

One evening Jake phoned that he was driving to Rapid City in the carryall and asked Margaret if she and Pat wanted to go along and select their bathroom fixtures. Margaret was relieved; she never had driven farther than Bison and was afraid the Ford wouldn't hold together on such a long trip.

Pat wanted to go. She wanted to do anything that would keep her mind away from Harmony, over in Mr. Lennox's stable, who was probably wondering why she didn't come and pick out his hoofs; but she secretly resented the way in which everything was arranged for her, the carpenters, the trip, the kind of material to buy, even the names of dealers who would show her special courtesy because she had been sent by Mr. Lennox. They were going through the motions of consulting her as though she were grownup, but actually treating her like a child.

When they reached Rapid City, Jake went to the feed store
to collect several bags of salt for the ranch and suggested that
they meet at four o'clock in the restaurant with the white horse
on its jukebox. After a hasty sandwich Margaret and Pat went
to a plumbing supply store and gazed with dazzled eyes at the
tiles, bathtubs, gleaming chromium racks.

"You choose," Margaret insisted, but Pat was firm.

"Oh no, Mummy, this is my present to you."

After Margaret had made her selection and they had come
away awed by the salesman's talk of sending a plumber to in-
stall the fixtures and supervise the building of the septic tank,
they wandered about the streets looking at the windows.

"We must think about your winter clothes," Margaret said
suddenly. Already the windows were full of autumn suits and
coats although the sun was still so hot that the pavements
burned through one's shoes.

"Do you like that green coat?" Margaret asked. It was fitted
slightly at the waist and looked as though it was intended to
be worn to church.

"Not for me, Mummy, I want something straighter and
simpler, but oh that hat would look lovely on you." She was
looking at a navy blue felt, a sailor with two red wings standing
smartly against the crown. Margaret stood enthralled before it.
Finally she took a step toward the door.

"You don't think it looks too frivolous? Maybe I'll try it on."

"While you do, I'd like to get Ma a present in the ten-cent
store. We'll meet at the White Horse."

Margaret hesitated for a moment then went resolutely
through the plate-glass door. Pat walked on down the street,
looking at everything and also keeping watch for the judge. She
and he had walked down this very street to the picture show
and any moment she expected to see him towering above the
river of people who swept by her, doffing his ten-gallon hat
right and left. On one of the office buildings she saw his name

shining in brass. She never had been in an office. Would he be annoyed if she called on him? If he was busy, she could always go away.

In the lobby, the directory on the wall told her that he was on the second floor. She climbed the stairs, walked down a corridor and found the door. It was open. Inside, a smartly-dressed young woman with rouged lips and hair in a smooth short wave was typing at a desk. "She's as sleek as Harmony," Pat thought, marveling at so much grooming.

The girl looked up and smiled.

"Well, young lady, what can we do for you?"

"I'd like to see the judge," Pat answered, stepping shyly inside.

"Business or pleasure?" The girl went on working while she spoke; her fingers hopped over the keys of the typewriter, without her looking at them, as though they had a life of their own.

"Er . . . personal, I guess."

"Then we'll call it pleasure. Come on in and sit down. The judge will be free in a minute."

Pat sat in one of the big leather chairs, and as she waited she began to feel uneasy. Maybe the judge would think she was foolish to bother him here. He might not feel like playing today; one couldn't have spring fever in August. But there she was; she couldn't get up and run away.

Just as she was almost ready to bolt for the stairs, the door of the inner office opened and a big rancher came out clutching his Stetson. He nodded to the girls and called back over his shoulder, "I'll do that, judge."

The girl jumped up from the typewriter and went into the inner office. A minute later she came out and said in a solemn voice, "The judge will see you." She waved Pat in and shut the door. The judge was sitting behind an enormous desk but even so, his head and shoulders dwarfed it.

"Well, if it isn't my little goddess of the springtime." The

judge towered over her and shook her hand. "That was some
pretty riding you did at the fair. How's the chestnut? Don't tell
me he has a shoe boil or you've fed him too many apples and
given him the colic. Are you going to enter him in any of the
big shows? You should, you know. He'd be a winner."

"But I can't. You see, I . . . I've sold Harmony."

The judge leaned forward, his eyes boring holes in her. Pat
felt the tears welling up into her eyes and batted her lashes to
keep from crying.

"Because you wanted to?" His eyes were as unblinking as
those of a snake. Pat couldn't get away from them.

"Well, yes. I . . . I guess so. We needed so many things. All
day we've been buying bathtubs and pink tile and chromium
fixtures, and every one of them makes me feel just as if I were
betraying Harmony."

"Who is *we?*"

"Mummy and I."

"Mmmm. Another mother fixation. Why do you come to
me?"

"Because I had been looking for you on the street and when
I saw your name downstairs I . . . Well, you were so nice to me."

The judge snorted.

"You needn't invent a reason. I know. You wanted someone
to tell you how noble and unselfish you are and what a magnificent thing you have done to sacrifice the creature you care
for most in the world for a few lengths of copper pipe and a
hot and cold water spigot. Well, I won't. Little girl, I'm going
to talk to you like a grown-up, and heaven help you if you
don't understand. You and you only are responsible for making
your life. Some people will help you, casually because they like
you and wish you well, others will harm you because they love
you and want you to have the things they value most. Your
mother wants you to have a bathtub and a new hat because she
wants them and therefore they are best for you. She is quite

sincere about it and yearns for you to have them. Doc loves
you. You are the apple of his sentimental old eye; I could tell
that when he gave you the blue ribbon. He is pushing you, too,
in the direction he honestly thinks you want to go. It probably
is, too, but be sure that it is what you want yourself, not a de-
sire that he has implanted in you."

The judge took off his glasses and waved them in her face.

"In other words, beware of those who love you. They are constantly assailing you. Be yourself, know what you want and go
after it. You don't need to hurt people along the way, on the
contrary, you can often help them. That isn't selfishness, it's
self-preservation. If horses are your great love, nothing else will
ever satisfy you and nothing will keep you from them for long,
but don't let yourself be sidetracked by the chance to make a
grandiloquent gesture.

"And if, by any chance, your heart traps you into making
one, let there be no regrets. Don't sulk, carry it off with a
flourish. The French have a word for it, 'panache,' carry your
plume high no matter what. Now then, mop the eyes. Panache,
I tell you, panache. Here endeth the first lesson."

The judge unwound himself from the desk and reached for
his Stetson.

"Now come and tell me who bought the horse and why—all
the grim details." He took her hand. As they crossed the outer
office he called to the girl at the reception desk, "We're going
over to the White Horse for a hot fudge sundae. Now don't look
at me like that. This is a conference."

Chapter 18

The Bargain

When Pat saw Margaret in the doorway, she blinked and looked again. Her mother was wearing the blue felt sailor with the red wings on it and a pair of navy pumps to match. Under her arm was a blue bag; the accessories made her tailored summer dress look strikingly white. She was like a picture stepping out of a fashion magazine. Behind her was Mr. Lennox. They saw Pat and came over to the booth in which she and the judge were considering a second round of sundaes. Mr. Lennox introduced Margaret. The judge stood up, eyeing her with appreciation.

"So this is why I couldn't find you. I had to fly over for a gasket, our water heater broke down, so I thought I might be able to help you about your plumbing fixtures. But I see you have expert legal advice."

The judge tossed his long white locks as he subsided onto his chair and rumbled at them in his deepest tones, "We have just finished our conference, sir. Will you join us in a sundae?"

They talked of the drought and prospects for a mild winter, of the advantages of Angus over Herefords, but neither mentioned Harmony. Pat began to breathe more easily, she couldn't have borne it if they had. When Jake came, Mr. Lennox said he would take Pat and Margaret home in the plane; he wanted to show them the badlands from the air. The judge shook hands all around, last of all with Pat.

"Well, goddess, I must return to toil. I can no longer pretend it's spring. I believe with Doc that your horoscope has some happy signs in it. And remember, no matter what, panache." He swept them all a good-by with his ten-gallon hat.

"Why does he call you goddess and what does he mean by 'panache'?" Mr. Lennox asked curiously.

"I don't know. It's just his way."

"Hmmm, seems to have taken quite a shine to you. He's clever as they make them."

Jake drove them to the airfield where a half-dozen Piper Cubs were scattered about like so many bugs. Mr. Lennox, Pat and Margaret climbed into the blue plane; Jake twirled the propeller. They taxied across the field, made a run and were off.

Pat in the back seat paid no attention to the conversation in front, she was sunk in her own thoughts. Doc, the judge—she was trying to figure out what they meant. At one moment everything was so clear; there was only the right or the wrong. If you did right you ought to be glad about it; you should be happy instead of sulky and resentful as she had been, there was no use pretending she hadn't. And then Doc and the judge came along and made you doubt that you were right after all; but even if you had done the mistaken thing, you should carry it off with a flourish. "Panache," she said the word over to herself, testing it on her lips. Did they mean that whatever she did or didn't do, she should stand up to the consequences and never let herself feel either smug or bitter inside? She was tired of thinking. Leaning her head against the side of the plane, she went to sleep.

"Mr. Lennox says Chet is going tomorrow morning," Margaret told Pat. "Don't you want to see them off?" Pat didn't want to go to the ranch. She didn't want to say good-by to Harmony in front of Ma and Ty and Jake, but by seven o'clock she was sitting on the culvert where the road and the lane met. The sun was not high yet and a little wind blew out of the west, riffling the dust. A sage hen sat under a clump of tumbleweed and watched the girl with unblinking eyes. She was so mottled and brown that Pat wouldn't have noticed her if the bird hadn't been in the direct line of her eyes. Presently a cloud of dust blew down the road. It was the big horse van. She stood up and waved.

Chet put on the brakes and jumped down, nervously, hoping there would be no tears.

"We're off. Wish us luck, kid, we're going to try to do you proud." He opened the back door and let her climb into the van. Harmony had heard her voice and turned his head toward her. He tossed it up and down and nuzzled her hand. She slipped a piece of sugar from her pocket and felt his lips reaching for it on the palm of her hand.

"How has he been, Chet? You know I couldn't bear to come over."

"A little off his feed. I think he misses you. Wish you were coming along."

Pat sighed, she rubbed the noses of Lady Luck and War Eagle and threw her arms for the last time around Harmony's neck, kissed his white star, then jumped to the road and helped Chet bolt the door.

"How will I know what luck you have?" she asked.

"Mr. Lennox will probably write to Ty or Ma, and if he doesn't, I'll send them clippings from the papers. Good-by, kid."

He climbed back into the cab and started the engine. "Be seeing you soon."

"Good-by." Pat sat down again on the culvert and burst into dry sobs.

The days slipped into one another. The carpenters had gone; the plumber came with a truckload of cesspool blocks and another of tiles and fixtures. While he laid the linoleum on the bathroom floor, the bathtub sat in the middle of the kitchen. Margaret groaned about the mess, but she was so fascinated with the bathroom that she watched every operation as though the man in the greasy overalls were a magician producing a rabbit from a hat. Pat was curious, too; she liked to know how things were done and talked to him while he cemented sheets of tile to a background of wire and plaster.

Almost every afternoon she walked over to Ty's, but it was over a week before there was news. Then a clipping came from Chet. Lady Luck had taken first in the skyscraper at Fort Wayne and another in the open; War Eagle, a third in the Handy Hunter Class; but there was no mention of Harmony at all. He must be sick, Pat thought. He must have a pulled tendon or had the colic or almost anything. He could outjump War Eagle any day.

"Jake, what do you think it means?" she asked. "You don't think Harmony's hurt or dead?"

"Of course not, we'd have heard. He isn't accustomed to campaigning. Maybe he just hasn't hit his stride."

There would be no more mail for another few days; it was useless to hang around waiting. Pat went with Margaret to Bison and found a room with a cousin of Jake whose daughter taught in the high school. The woman was friendly and comfortable to be with and said she would look after Pat. They even went to a movie and had dinner in the quick-lunch restaurant, the only one in town.

The next day the plumber finished his work. Margaret scrubbed the kitchen and washed the last speck of dust and cement from the pink tile walls that circled the bathroom, halfway to the ceiling on the high end and all the way on the low one where the lean-to ceiling sloped down. That was the end in which the carpenter had put a little casement window. The tub stood under it; one could lie in it and see clear to the buttes. It was going to be fun to take a bath on a broiling summer day.

Margaret pushed back the damp hair from her face and standing in the kitchen door threw the last bucketful of scrubbing water as far as she could fling it. The thirsty ground soaked it up with scarcely a damp spot to mark where it had fallen.

"Now," she said to Pat, hanging up the scrubbing rag, "you take the first bath. Here is a cake of scented-pine soap, the last that Sketch sent us." Her face clouded. How like Sketch; he had given her the luxurious soap, but never the bath.

"I'd rather you would, Mummy. It's my present." She had almost said, "It was my Harmony." She thought it, but at the same time she thought, "panache," and the bitterness did not seep into her voice. It had power; it was a magical word.

"Here," she gave the soap to Margaret. "Shall I turn on the gas under the tank? Do you want to wait until the water's hot?"

"Yes, turn it on; but I want one right now. I don't mind how cold it is." Margaret turned on the water in the tub and ran into her room for a thick white beachrobe that Sketch had given her; she never had worn it for it was much too hard to keep clean. She closed the door. Pat heard her splashing in the water, catching her breath and laughing. Presently she came out in the white robe, her face rosy and her feet leaving wet imprints on the floor. She laid her damp cheek against Pat's.

"I don't know how to thank you. I think you really must love me very much."

She did, she did; but couldn't Margaret see it was half for

Sketch, half because she wanted to take up the responsibilities that he had left. Nobody ever understood what went on in another person's heart.

September spun itself out in endless days. Pat haunted Ty's. She was embarrassed to appear so anxious so she stayed down by the gate to watch for the postman.

"What are you looking for, honey, a letter from your sweetheart? Not a thing for you today." She could hardly wait until he had gone to snatch the bundle for Ty and run to the house. Mostly the mail was just the weekly paper from Bison, letters to Mr. Lennox, bills, advertisements, but one day there would be a fat envelope from Chet. When it came, Jake let her rip it open and read the clippings first. Lady Luck was riding high, blue ribbon after blue ribbon, and War Eagle often picked up a red one or a yellow, but never a mention of Harmony. Once in Columbus he won a fourth prize, but that was all. Pat couldn't understand it. Jake couldn't either, but he tried to comfort her. Mr. Lennox would bring the horses to Kansas City at the end of the first week in October to let them rest up for the American Royal, then they would hear. But Pat was going to school in Bison the first of the month, how would she know?

"I'll drive over and bring you home for that first weekend," he promised. "There are things I want to do in Bison anyway."

Getting ready for school helped and so did riding around with Doc. His confidence in Harmony was not shaken.

"If ever I saw a jumper in my life, and believe me, it has been a long one full of them, that horse has the makings of a champion. Six weeks haven't changed him. He may be sick, he may have had an accident that would have kept him out of the ring; but, whatever it is, we'll hear from him yet. Chin up, little one. Don't you worry."

"You and the judge," she tried to laugh and managed a convincing smile. " 'Panache,' that's his magic word and it's mine too."

" 'Panache'? How like the judge. We'll be saying it together. See, you're feeling braver right away."

The house in which Pat was to live in Bison was only two doors from Doc's office. Margaret drove Pat over on Sunday afternoon. Her own school was opening on Monday and Pat had helped her clean the blackboards and wash the windows.

"This year I'm not afraid," Margaret said, "but I never could have done it last year if it hadn't been for you."

Pat's first week of school was confusing; so many pupils, so many teachers, a different one for each subject. Bob and his cousins from the little school in the buttes were her only friends, but it wasn't long until everyone was calling her Pat and inviting her to play on the school teams. In the afternoons when Doc was at home he took her to the one soda fountain and treated Bob and any of her friends who happened to be around.

On Friday afternoon she waited for Jake; she was so tense that she couldn't stay in her room, but walked up and down the street watching for his car. But it wasn't Jake who came, it was Mr. Lennox with Margaret. She was wearing the new hat and shoes with her pale blue flannel suit and she looked as perfect as the lovely mannikins in the Rapid City shop windows. Mr. Lennox took them to the ice cream parlor for a sundae.

"I wish there were some place I could take you for dinner, a place worthy of Margaret's pretty costume, but there just isn't. We should have come in the plane, then we could have hopped over to Rapid City."

But Margaret insisted they go home as she had dinner practically ready. They talked about Mr. Lennox's house that was almost done, endlessly discussing the material for the curtains and the heavy rustic chairs that he was sending from Kansas City. Pat listened with her heart beating a tattoo against her ribs. She wanted to interrupt, to ask about Harmony, but Mr. Lennox and Margaret were so absorbed in each other that it was as though they were surrounded by a wall of glass; she could see them, but she couldn't break through.

It was almost dark when they left Bison. At the Cole house, Mr. Lennox built up the fire while Margaret changed into a gingham dress. The fire filled the room with comfort for the nights were already chilly.

"Mr. Lennox," Pat said hastily before Margaret came back and she was shut out again, "tell me about Harmony. Is he sick? Didn't you show him? What happened to him?"

Mr. Lennox sat down at the table and ran his hands through his crisp blond hair.

"I wish I didn't have to tell you, Pat. Harmony has let us down. I thought he was going to be a great jumper, but he just doesn't stand up to it. He can jump, there is no question about that, but he's too indifferent; he hasn't the heart, the determination to win that makes a good show horse. I'm sorry, child. It's a disappointment, but sometimes things do turn out that way."

"I can't believe it. He has courage, he isn't afraid of anything. Ask Chet, he's seen me jump him five feet, clean as a whistle and room to spare."

"I know. Chet's just as puzzled about it as I am."

"What are you going to do with him?"

"Sell him, I guess, at the sales after the Kansas City show. It's no use keeping a horse that's second-rate."

"Sell him!" Pat stood up and clenched her hands to keep from crying. "But you can't sell Harmony. I'd never see him again." She walked over to the man sitting by the kitchen table and stood before him with wide, tear-bright eyes.

"Will you sell Harmony back to me? I know I haven't any money now, but when I get out of school I'll work and make it somehow. I'll pay you back every penny."

"Don't be foolish, Pat." Margaret had come unnoticed into

the kitchen and was spreading a cloth on the table. "Don't you know that you're really asking Mr. Lennox to give you the horse. He must get what he can for Harmony. Even so, he will have lost money on the horse."

Mr. Lennox put his hand over Margaret's to still her.

"If you had him again, Pat, what would you do with him?"

"I'd ride him in the shows and make you see how good he is. Maybe he misses me and Tip. Maybe he won't jump for anyone else but me."

"That could be," Mr. Lennox admitted thoughtfully.

"Is he entered in the American Royal?"

"Yes, Chet wanted him to have one more chance, but I don't think it's any use. If you could have seen him walking through the shows at Detroit and Fort Wayne! It was just by accident that he got a third. Not a spark, nothing to catch your imagination."

Pat had not moved; she was still looking at him with enormous solemn eyes, ignoring Margaret.

"Let me ride him in Kansas City. If he wins a blue ribbon, will you sell him to me? If not, then you can take him to the auction. Please let me try. Harmony and I, we believe in each other."

"We're getting far too serious." Mr. Lennox shook his head, laughing. "This was going to be a party. Margaret, will you let her go to Kansas City? If she wins, I'll give her Harmony and see that she has a chance to ride him in every horse show in the country, if she wants to. My cousin has a large apartment, plenty of room for Pat, and she'd love to look after her. We can do that much for Pat, can't we?"

Margaret sat down beside him at the table and leaned her lovely dark head on her hands. She too was looking at him, and Pat could see that she was melting.

"Whatever you want."

Jumping up quickly, she began to rattle the pans on the stove.

"Will you set the table, Pat?" she said without turning around.

Pat was stunned. The room was charged with emotion, hers, her mothers—she felt as though she were being sucked into a whirlpool. Mr. Lennox was the only stable one. She gave him her hand and he held it tight. Her heart was singing so loud that it drummed in her ears. She wished Doc were here and the judge who had believed that things would work out right if she held onto her courage.

"Panache," she muttered softly.

"What did you say, dear?" Margaret asked.

"Nothing, Mummy, nothing at all."

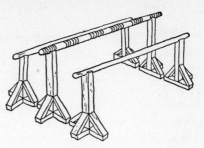

Chapter 19

I Give You My Word

After dinner Mr. Lennox brought from his car a program of the American Royal show and opened it on the table.

"I want to show you what you're up against. These are the courses." Pat and Margaret leaned over the page of oval diagrams marked with arrows and dotted lines and indications of the various jumps. "There isn't one of these jumps that Harmony hasn't taken. We have most of them here except the Hog's Back and the Double-Crossed Poles. I've entered him in the Warmup, the Knockdown and Out and the Touch and Out. If you win a first in any of these you'll have saved your horse, but I think the chances are about one in a thousand. Look at me, Pat. I don't want any heartbroken tragedy queen on my hands. Have you the courage to take it if you don't win a thing?"

"Honest," Pat assured him. "I give you my word."

The rest of the evening they spent making plans. Mr. Lennox would not be returning until the next week-end, so Pat would miss five days of school; but he thought seeing all of the horse show, the first big one, would be worth it to her.

"Isn't there any way you could manage to come along, a substitute or something?" he asked Margaret. She could see no way. To get a substitute for anything as frivolous as a horse show

would discredit her forever in the eyes of the school board. She
was doubtful about Pat's going alone even with the assurance
that Mr. Lennox and Chet would look after her. Pat never had
seen Kansas City or a real horse show and might be lost and
overwhelmed. She was just a child. But Margaret had given
them her word; the matter was out of her hands.

The first class in which Harmony was entered was scheduled
for a Sunday matinee. They had to start off by noon the next
day as the Navion was not equipped for night flying. When Mr.
Lennox left it was late and both Pat and Margaret were tired.

"You're so excited, you'll never sleep," Margaret said. She
heated a cup of milk for Pat and shooed her to bed.

In the morning, Pat and her mother washed and ironed and
packed. The habit and cap already were in the gay boxes in
which they had come. The boots were troublesome; they took
up almost all the room in Sketch's cowhide bag, crowding the
jeans and gingham blouses.

"I wish you had some pretty clothes, sweet. If there had been
time we could have found something."

But Pat was not concerned with clothes; she would do well
enough in her beret and school coat.

When the Navion swooped down in the front pasture, Pat
was ready. Margaret brought out the boxes, Mr. Lennox the
suitcase; they shoved the baggage behind the seats. He walked
back with Margaret to the house to tell her good-by. Tip came
yelping from the barn and leaped up on Pat, trying to lick her
hand.

"Funny face, you know where I'm going? If Harmony could
only have you! He's lonely without his mascot," Pat said softly.
And why not? She was daring a great deal anyway. When Mr.
Lennox returned, Pat was in her seat with Tip in her lap. Be-
fore he could say a word, Pat burst out, "See how little Tip is.
He won't be in anybody's way. And he's Harmony's mascot.

I GIVE YOU MY WORD   [183]

Don't you think Harmony ought to have every encouragement we can give him? He hasn't anything to try for if he doesn't find Tip in his stall when he comes back."

Mr. Lennox burst out laughing.

"You are the darnedest kid. But keep him on your side in case he gets airsick. He's your responsibility. I expect Chet can help you look after him."

They were off. Pat looked back, swallowing a lump in her throat as Margaret waved. At first she kept her face turned to the window, looking down on the prairie flowing underneath, but after a while her head began to nod. When they came down at Pierre for gas she lifted Tip out stiffly and flexed her knees. The man with the hose leaned down to pull Tip's ears and rub his back.

"He'll get along," Mr. Lennox said. "He has such winning ways. I didn't know Harmony had a mascot. Lady Luck once made friends with a chicken, a scrawny little gray hen, and when the hen died she was off her feed for weeks. Maybe you and Tip are just what Harmony needs."

The rest of the way Pat watched the map below her. The prairie was greener, more corn and wheat fields, and the farms were blocked off like checkerboards with the houses and barns in one corner next to the road. At the Kansas City airport Chet met them with a car. He didn't seem to be surprised at seeing Pat.

"Hello, kid," he greeted her. "I thought you might make it somehow."

Everything was so confusing, the large airliners coming in and taking off, porters rushing about with hand trucks and crowds of people milling around the gates, that Pat clung to Mr. Lennox's arm and gripped Tip so hard that he whimpered.

They had alighted in the heart of the city. As Chet turned the car into a main street, all the buildings and people seemed to be jumping at Pat. Yet the city was beautiful beyond her dreams, when the lights came on and the street windows flashed by like strings of jewels.

The car stopped in front of an apartment building, impressive enough to be the state capitol. Mr. Lennox understood that Pat would be confused by doormen and elevators so he took her by the hand. The apartment itself was as big as a house, with gleaming furniture and rugs as soft as turf. The cousin, Mrs. Trent, was as sleek as the actresses in the movies, but she was friendly and put Pat at her ease. Mr. Lennox stayed for supper, dinner they called it, and afterward drove Pat to the stables. The stalls were in the stockyard, he said.

They walked along a row of boxes from which inquiring heads stuck out, hunters, saddle horses and ponies, all entered in the show. War Eagle, Lady Luck and Harmony were side by side. The light was dim, but Pat could see Harmony's white star on the long head sticking out of the stall; his ears pricked forward. Tip who had raced ahead of her, was already in the stall, dashing about with a joyful racket. Harmony nuzzled him, cornered him and snorted in mock ferocity the way they used to play; then whirled about and rubbed his nose against Pat's back, so happy that he had to be bobbing his head and rubbing against them both at once. She threw her arms around his neck and kissed him between the eyes.

"Don't you think I'd better stay with him tonight? He likes to have me in his stall."

"It would simplify things if she wants to," Chet said. "We've got to get to work at about five in the morning."

"Very well, will you drive her back to the apartment for her jeans? I'll see that Ed gives the horses their supper. Ed . . . Where's that fellow?"

A lanky boy came out of War Eagle's stall chewing a straw and slouched against the door as he listened to Mr. Lennox. As they drove off, Chet explained that he had to have help at the big shows. The large exhibitors were out to win. Most of their horses were ridden by professionals and all in all, it didn't do to leave your horses alone for a single moment.

When they returned, Chet showed Pat the tack stall in which two cots were set against the side walls. It was a neat little room full of saddles and bridles and smelled of harness soap and metal polish.

"I could have another cot put in here," he said, "or Ed could sleep in the stall with Lady Luck." But Pat wanted to be with Harmony. Chet understood; he spread several blankets on clean straw in a corner of the stall. Pat settled down on them and pretended to be asleep, but Harmony wouldn't quiet down; every few minutes he wheeled to poke his nose into Pat's back or nuzzle Tip. Finally she decided it would be better to leave him alone for a while; she slipped out of the stall and found Chet in front of the tack stall playing solitaire in the dim light.

"What do you think was the matter with Harmony?" Pat asked him. "Tell me honestly, why didn't he jump?"

Chet took off his cap and scratched his head.

"Blessed if I know, Pat. He wasn't sick or lame, he just wasn't interested. He'd jump all right when I put him at them; he'd get over, but he didn't care how. He didn't give that extra something. You know the way Lady Luck ducks her head in embarrassment when she touches or doesn't do her best. Well, Harmony doesn't care how many rails he knocks down. He's lost all his pride, his style. It's been just like he's dragging around a heart of pig iron. I honestly think he's just homesick for you."

"Then you believe we might have a chance tomorrow? You know if we don't win, Mr. Lennox is going to sell him after the show."

Chet didn't answer right away; he carefully put a black four on a red five, then looked her hard in the eyes.

"Yes, I do. He'll jump for you and he *can* jump; but this is a

big show, the judges will have no mercy with their faulting.
You'll be up against twenty or thirty of the best horses in the
country, old-timers, most of them, and ridden by experts who
know how to get the most out of them. I think it depends on
you. And now you get some sleep. I mean sleep. We've got to
be up around five."

He took Pat by the shoulder and pushed her gently into the
stall. Harmony had been watching them. When Pat rubbed his
nose, he turned his head to the wall, lay down and contentedly
went to sleep. Pat drew a blanket over herself. Tip curled up
against her. He was nervous; he twitched at the stockyard
noises, the bellowing of cattle and the grunting of sheep and
pigs. Pat shut her eyes tight, willing herself to sleep.

When she awoke it was not quite light. Chet was moving
about in the next stall, calling Ed. Pat jumped up and brushed
the straw from her hair. She stepped out of the stall. About her,
shadowy figures were moving. In the half-light she heard the
clinking of water buckets and the stomping of wakened horses.
Ed brought a pail each for Chet and Pat; his long arms with the
buckets at the ends of them looking like those of some giant ape.
When they had crosstied their horses and groomed them it was
full daylight. Pat could see what her ears had been telling her,
that all along the row of stalls horses were being shined and
polished for the show. By seven o'clock War Eagle, Lady Luck
and Harmony were back in their freshly-cleaned stalls, their
sleek coats covered by cotton dust blankets.

"Scrub up," Chet said. "Ed will watch them while we go and
eat."

They went to a diner up the street, ate breakfast and drank
coffee with the other trainers. Even though Pat did not like
coffee it was so hot and comforting that she put her chilly
fingers around the cup and drank the coffee. She sat by Chet, a
little apart from the others, and listened to him gossiping with
them, boasting about Lady Luck's record and speculating on

her chances of taking the championship. But they were all boasting, leaning on the counter in the early sunshine, their caps
pushed back. Pat wished one of them would mention Harmony.
She wanted to ask them, "Have you noticed the big chestnut in
our stall? You just watch him jump this afternoon."

When she realized that it was actually this afternoon, she
was seized with panic. It was here, her chance and Harmony's,
the chance Sketch had talked about. Would he be proud of her?
He had ridden here, maybe his parade horse and cutting horse
had occupied these very stalls. She felt him closer to her than
he had been since the night he sat beside her on the corral fence
and told her he would never leave her.

Chet finished his second cup of coffee and motioned to her. By
the time they had braided the horses' manes and tails, Mr. Lennox had come. He tilted up Pat's chin.

"Happy?"

She grinned at him, too speechless to thank him.

Several jumps were set up in the ring, he said. Fifteen or
twenty horses and riders were gathering in the ring of the
American Royal building, professional riders like Chet, a few
amateurs, one or two women, slim and assured. Pat stuck close
to Chet. Mr. Lennox gave her a leg up on Harmony and they
went up the ramp. Perhaps a dozen riders already were taking
their horses over the jumps.

Pat reined up next to Chet.

"Watch a few minutes," he suggested. "See how the professionals work their horses."

"Chet, look. What's that?" She grasped his arm and pointed
to a trainer and a groom who were working a handsome black
horse at a four-foot rail. As the horse rose to clear the rail, the
groom rapped his front legs with a heavy pole, making him
jump a little higher. When he came down, tossing his head,
snorting and trying to get away, Pat watched with troubled
questioning eyes.

"The tape that's wrapped around the end of the pole is filled with tacks with their points sticking out. They're filed down but even so, they sometimes draw blood. I wouldn't use a pole on a horse. The bamboo pole is better. Like the one that man over there is using. They don't hurt much, but they make a lot of noise."

Pat blinked her eyes and her lashes were wet.

"Did you use it on Harmony?"

"It didn't hurt him. I had to do everything I could think of to try to liven him up. Go on, walk him around a bit and show him the jumps before you try one."

Pat dropped her eyes. She didn't want to look at Chet. She felt betrayed. No wonder Harmony wouldn't jump.

"It's all right, honey," Pat said soothingly. "You know I wouldn't do anything like that to you. Come on now, pet, let's show them what you can do." Harmony tossed his head. He went at the first rail unwillingly, as though he dreaded it. He made it clean. Pat stroked him and praised him, gave him a lump of sugar, then rode him around again before she tried another. Under the praise he brightened up. When he understood that no one was going to hit him, he was in high spirits and took the next jump with a flourish. As he cantered back around the ring he tossed his head proudly, as much as to say, "Well, how was that?" Pat kissed him on his star and Mr. Lennox stroked his withers. Harmony loved it and turned his head from side to side, looking for further admiration.

Mr. Lennox's friends came by and spoke to him. One girl, not much older than Pat, rode by on a handsome white mare. Her jeans were as dusty as Pat's and there was a smudge on her nose; but there was an air of assurance about her as though she had lived at horse shows all her life. She stooped over and patted Harmony's neck.

"Hello," she called to Mr. Lennox. "I see you have a new rider."

Mr. Lennox led Pat over to the white mare.

"This is Pat Cole and she can ride the hide off a bronco. You'll have to look out for your laurels."

The girl thrust out her hand and Pat shyly took it.

"I've been watching you. You're great. If you spoil my chances for the jumper stake, I'll cut your throat." She waved and cantered away. Pat watched her take the jumps. Her form was perfect and the mare flew over the bars like a silver arrow. Pat clenched her hands.

"Chet, is she better than Harmony?"

"She's good, almost the best. She and Lady Luck fight it out in every class in which they meet, but you're not afraid of Lady Luck. Don't be afraid of her."

Chapter 20

Matinee

When they had finished the morning workout, Mr. Lennox took Pat to his cousin's apartment for lunch. The jumper class was the first one scheduled for the matinee so there was not too much time. When Mrs. Trent saw Pat she gave a little mock cry of horror.

"My dear, how did you ever manage to get so filthy? Go to the bathroom and scrub yourself. You might as well put on your riding habit before lunch. Use the violet bath salts and plenty of toilet water." Mrs. Trent turned on the bath, dumping in a generous handful of salts that filled the room with a delicate perfume.

"Here is the powder and there is the toilet water. Have a grand soaking."

Pat felt somehow disgraced. She couldn't help getting dirty in the stable. But as she soaked in luxury, inhaling the perfume of the violet salts, her embarrassment vanished. Finally, she stepped out of the bath and dried herself on a towel thicker and softer than any she ever had seen. She put on her riding habit, smoothed the coat, tied her stock carefully the way Doc had showed her and came back shyly into the living room. Now she was spotless and there was not a particle of dust on her, not even on the shining boots.

Mrs. Trent looked her over.

"Why, Paul, she's a darling. Come into my room a minute." She led Pat to her dressing table and dusted her face with powder.

"There now, you practically scrubbed the skin off."

When they returned Mr. Lennox glanced at Pat with approval.

"You're a different girl when you get the straw out of your hair."

After lunch, Mrs. Trent said that she and Pat would be at the show in plenty of time. Mr. Lennox needn't wait. Pat watched her hostess dress. Never had she seen so many bottles and jars, so many perfumes, rouges and creams. It took as long to dress with all these as it did to groom a horse, and when Mrs. Trent was finished she looked just as sleek and perfect; but Pat had to clench her hands to keep from fidgeting. She thought they would never get started.

Mrs. Trent smiled at Pat as she put a touch of mascara on her eyelashes.

"Now we're ready. Will I do?"

Pat nodded shyly.

"That's the best grooming I ever saw."

The woman laughed and smoothed Pat's velvet cap.

"That's the right angle. You look pretty sweet yourself."

At last they were starting; Mrs. Trent collected her coat and gloves, but she stopped to put a drop of perfume behind each ear. Pat was already halfway down the hall. She felt that she would explode if she didn't get back to Harmony.

They drove fast; Pat didn't need to silently urge Mrs. Trent on. At the American Royal building she took Pat down to Chet and Mr. Lennox where the jumpers were gathering beneath the

ring. Ed was holding Harmony. The horse flicked his ears at
Pat and his big eyes glowed when she kissed his star. It was almost time. Mr. Lennox told her to go up and get her starting
number from the man at the gate. "Seventeen." She was the
last one. Chet, shined and scrubbed, waited on Lady Luck at
the foot of the ramp where the early numbers were gathered—
a beautiful lot of horses with their satin coats and their rows of
clubbed pigtails lying smooth on their necks. The girl on the
white mare waved to Pat. She was number one and she sat so
trim and glowing, her eyes dancing with excitement, that Pat
felt all of her shyness and anxiety melt away.

"Pat, honey." She took her eyes from the golden girl and
looked over her shoulder. It was Doc, unfamiliar and somehow
imposing in tweeds.

"You look very elegant." He admired her smooth plaits and
the way she had tied her stock. "Remember, don't pay any attention to the crowd. Don't even look at them. Just think of
Harmony. Your job is to relax and feel sure of yourself so you
can give him confidence. And don't let him break pace after
you head for the first jump. Breaking pace from a canter is a
fault this year. Are you sure you know the course?"

The bugle sounded. Doc kissed Pat on the cheek for luck and
said he was going up to watch. The girl on the white mare was
at the gate. The rumble of voices died to a murmur as she rode
into the course. Pat listened, trying to tell by the murmur of
the crowd whether there were any faults. The girl came back
radiant.

"She went clean," she said. Jumping down from the mare the
girl patted her and gave her a lump of sugar. The mare was
proud of herself, tossing her head and looking around like an
actress ready to take a curtain call.

"Number two. Number three." They moved along quickly.
Sometimes they were scarcely in the ring before the bugle
hustled them out. The clattering of rails punctuated the rumb-

ling murmur of the crowd. "Number thirteen." Chet, who was fourteen, moved up on Lady Luck.

Now they were in the ring. Mr. Lennox had gone up to watch; Pat was alone and suddenly appalled by the vastness, the noise and the strangers all around. She concentrated on what was happening above, trying to make her ears answer for her eyes. Lady Luck would go clean, she knew it. A few minutes later the staccato burst of applause told her so. Lady Luck came through the gate dancing with prideful little steps, craning her neck for applause. Chet slipped down, gave her to Ed and came over to Pat.

"All ready?"

Number sixteen had gone in but he didn't last longer than a few jumps. Someone said he had been disqualified for three refusals. Chet smiled up at Pat.

"Good luck, kid."

Mr. Lennox who had come back, walked with her to the ramp. "Take your time. Don't let him rush his fences."

"Number seventeen."

Pat stroked Harmony's neck as the gate drew back for them. Entering the auditorium with its tiers of blurred and chattering faces was something like the shock of coming out of a cellar into the full sun. She blinked and caught her breath; then she shut out the faces and concentrated on the jumps.

Harmony tensed up; she felt his power as he circled the end of the ring, but he was confused as though he wasn't quite sure what she wanted him to do.

"See, these jumps aren't so bad," she whispered to him as they passed. "We can do them. We've done higher ones, honey. Let's show them." She was talking to him for her sake as well as his, trying to give them both confidence.

They started down the course.

"Steady, fellow, don't rush," she whispered as they approached the first jump. But he laid back his ears and instead of taking off on a curve, jumped straight up and down as though he were making a terrific effort. Yet, somehow, he cleared. The gate did not slow him down. At the far end of the course he changed leads correctly for the run down the middle. Now the Hog's Back. This Pat dreaded for Harmony didn't like it. He didn't mind the height—it was only four feet—but this jump with the middle rail higher than the other two, seemed to arouse his hostility. Twice during the morning workout he had refused, but now he snorted and charged it, taking both it and the Oxer as though they were three-foot rails. Coming back, he negotiated the Railroad Gate and the Post and Rails with his forefeet tucked in nicely. That was better; he was feeling more confident. Now the Hog's Back again and the Oxer. Would he clear them this time? Would their luck hold?

"Honey, you know what depends on it," she pleaded. "I couldn't stand it if I had to give you up."

The thought of what would happen if they failed, she had kept shut in a hidden corner of her mind; but it surged back over her and filled her with panic. She tried to control herself before Harmony felt her desperation. They were taking off for the Hog's Back. If he had a knockdown it would be her fault because she had doubted him.

Harmony took the Hog's Back as though he were gloating over an enemy. Now the Oxer remained. Pat called to Harmony, "This is it, this is the last." Then it happened. Harmony took off too close to the jump and ticked the high rail of the Oxer with his hind foot. A half fault! Pat realized it with a sick constriction of her stomach. She rode him out of the ring with her head sunk into her stock.

Chet and Mr. Lennox were waiting for her. Mr. Lennox held up his arms and Pat slid into them. He gave her a mighty hug.

"That was a beautiful exhibition, child. Don't worry about the tick. It wasn't Harmony's fault, he just isn't accustomed to you yet. This is the best he's done, the kind of jumping I expected of him. I'm proud as punch of both of you. I'll enter him in the Jumper Stake; he deserves a try for the big prize."

Pat glanced up at him. He really meant it; he wasn't just being kind. He put his arm around her.

"Come on, let's watch the jump-off."

Lady Luck was one of the four who had gone clean and so was the white mare of the golden girl, but Pat was still quivering so hard that she couldn't move. Mr. Lennox gave her an understanding smile and went into the ring without her. She leaned against Harmony and collapsed inside; the strength oozed out of her.

For a long time she stood there dazed, not feeling, not thinking, just trying to breathe, until she was aroused by a roar of cheering from the ring. Somebody put his hand on her arm. It was Doc and the tips of his moustache were pointing up in a broad smile.

"That's for Lady Luck. She won the blue ribbon. And you, little one, made a fine showing. Harmony isn't sure of you yet. He'll do better every day. In the morning why don't you take him into the ring early and ride him bareback without a bridle, the way you used to do? That will give him the feel of you again. I'll come down and watch you."

Pat's eyes spilled over.

"That's my girl. A regular splashing fountain. Don't you ever have a handkerchief?" Doc laughed as he reached for a carefully-folded square in his breast pocket.

Chapter 21

Rodeo

The next morning Doc was in the ring when Pat and Harmony arrived, the chestnut shining like velvet and handsomer than ever without saddle and bridle. The horse gave Doc a friendly nudge.

"You see, the strangeness is wearing off. He knows he's with friends again."

The jumps had been set up. Doc removed Harmony's halter and Pat tied a piece of binder twine around the horse's neck. Doc gave her a leg up, and Harmony was off, responding so quickly to the pressure of her knees that she barely touched the cord. He cantered happily around the ring, stretching his neck and snorting like a colt in pasture. She circled him several times, then rode back and forth, feeling him change his leads smoothly. By the time she had swung him into a figure eight she had forgotten Doc, everything except the delight of being at one again with Harmony. The jumps were without wings, but he didn't run out, he took them straight, eagerly, sharing her excitement.

Finally, when both the horse and girl were deliciously tired and winded, Pat jumped off in front of Doc, who was watching her from the judges' stand. Beside him sat a brisk and tweedy gentleman whom she had not noticed. Doc introduced him as the manager of the show. Pat gave him a moist, grubby hand, but her eyes were all for Doc.

"Didn't he do well? Don't you think he's going better? He didn't refuse once and he likes it."

"Just a minute, Pat." Doc told her that one of the exhibition riders who had expected to appear in the matinee for crippled children had broken his arm and couldn't ride. The manager wanted her to give an exhibition of bareback riding—just what she had been doing.

"It will be a great experience for you both, and you can't get too much before the Knockdown and Out tomorrow night."

Pat looked doubtfully at the manager.

"Do you think we're good enough?"

"Yes, I do. Wear just what you have on, stick a few straws in your pigtails, and we'll announce you as the Dakota cowgirl."

Doc and the manager walked off, and Pat put her arms around Harmony who nuzzled her shoulder.

"What do you think of that, old starface. Come on and walk before you get stiff. We have to put on a show this afternoon."

Back at the stalls, Pat tried to keep her mind on Harmony's tack which she was polishing for the next class. Chet and Ed were working too. Chet was so proud of her and Harmony that he spread the news about the exhibition up and down the stalls. As he settled back to work he kept talking about that little pacing mule he never could forget.

"I was lying to you, Pat, when I told you there'd be other horses to take the place of Harmony. It was for your own good, understand, when I thought you were going to lose him; but there never is another like the first one. I couldn't even love Lady Luck the way I loved that Jenny."

"But I haven't got Harmony. He's entered in only two more classes, the Knockdown and Out and the Jumper Stake and you know he hasn't a chance at the stake. You told me he'll have to face the winners of all the jumping classes and you can't expect him to take the biggest prize in the show. Chet, my heart falls down to my socks every time I think about it."

"Oh, you can't tell. The Stake isn't so much harder than the others. You'll get a first, honey. Something tells me you will. You just gotta believe in yourself."

Chet hung up the bridle upon which he had been working as he saw Mr. Lennox and his cousin coming between the stalls. Mrs. Trent was making a mocking little grimace at the smell of manure and saddle leather.

"Wash your face, my dear," she said to Pat. "We're taking you out to lunch and then we're going shopping. I'm giving a supper party Saturday night after the Jumper Stake, and we're going to find you a lovely dress to wear."

"But it . . . I can't go this afternoon. I'm going to be in the exhibition for the crippled children. The manager asked me."

"Paul, did you hear that? Pat is making her debut as a rodeo star."

Mr. Lennox put an arm around Pat's shoulders.

"Chet has been telling me. I didn't know you and Harmony could do exhibition bareback riding and I'm terribly proud of you, chick. The shopping can be put off until Wednesday— you're not riding then. I expect you'd rather stay right here than go out to lunch, wouldn't you? We'll be back in time for the show."

"Good guy," Chet said, looking after Mr. Lennox. "I don't know about the dame. Sorta chi-chi, ain't she?"

"Not really when you know her. She's been awfully nice to me." Pat hung up her bridle and looked anxiously into Harmony's stall where he was napping, with Tip rolled up in his feed box.

"Can I lunch with you, Chet? I'm so excited that I don't want anything but a glass of milk and a doughnut."

When the exhibition riders gathered around the ramp at two o'clock, Pat's nervousness began to melt away. This was going to be fun. There was none of the tenseness, the grimness that she had felt before the warmup. With no ribbons to win, all of them were laughing, clowning, prepared to give the children a circus to remember.

"Hello, cowgirl. Nice straw you're wearing." A big clown with red splotches on his face trotted over to her on a pony that, he said, could do everything except talk. From the ring they could hear the excited voices of the children.

Pat was third, after the clown and the mule that jumped through a hoop of fire and knelt like a camel. She and Harmony couldn't do funny tricks; but she stuck out her pigtails as straight as they would go, and pinned on her blouse the sunflower that Mr. Lennox had given her.

"Pat Cole, the cowgirl from Dakota and the horse she saved from death." The announcer was telling the children about Harmony and his mother, about the bitter winter in the buttes and the starved colt that was scarcely worth gunpowder. When they entered the ring, the children cheered and clapped until her eardrums ached. She and Harmony cantered around the ring close to the rail where the children could see him, so much at ease that she could pick out individual faces; the little girl with her arm in a cast and the dark-faced boy in braces who kept his eyes fastened on her so desperately and intently that he didn't even smile.

The figure eights the children loved; when she took the jumps, clinging to Harmony like an Indian with her thighs and knees and white socked feet, they spluttered with delight. After the jumps, which Harmony skimmed over as though he were a sailboat, Pat rode close by the box in which the solemn-eyed boy was sitting and tossed the sunflower into his lap. She glanced back over her shoulder as she left the ring and saw that he was smiling as he clutched the flower.

Pat tossed the sunflower into his lap.

The next afternoon when the entries gathered for the Knock-down and Out, Pat did not feel like a stranger. The girl on the white mare asked her what Harmony had done in the Warmup. Other riders smiled and nodded to her; Chet and Mr. Lennox were not so careful to keep her under their wing. This time she knew Harmony would have to go clean to stand a chance in the jump-off, for there would surely be two or three who would take the course without a knockdown.

Harmony thought he was giving another exhibition; he sailed over the jumps with gusto, enjoying every one of them. The strain was gone. It was as though he and Pat were having a morning workout in the pasture. The audience caught his spirit and gave him a rousing cheer.

Lady Luck, the white mare, a handsome bay under a professional rider and Harmony were in the jump-off. Harmony took the four foot six jumps without trouble and so did Lady and the white. But the bay, goaded by rough poling before the jump-off, reared and bolted. With only the three horses left to jump, the course was again raised three inches.

"Certainly getting up there, aren't they, fellow?" Pat whispered to Harmony. "We'll have to do our best and then some to win this ribbon."

Lady Luck and the white mare went clean so it was now Harmony's turn.

"Come on, old dear, we can do it too." It seemed as though Harmony understood for as he gathered himself together, she could feel the beautiful rhythm of his muscles clear up through her spine. He took the first five jumps handily, but in his eagerness he got in too close on the sixth and his hind hoof caught the rail.

The next time Lady Luck went clean and the white mare had a knockdown on the third fence. Outside of the ring the golden girl gave Pat a hug.

"You have a grand horse. If you keep on riding like this, I'll have to slit your throat before the show is over."

Mr. Lennox was so happy that he lifted Pat clear off the floor and swung her around.

"But Harmony didn't get the blue ribbon," she reminded him.

"Never mind." He set her back on the tan bark. "That was a beautiful exhibition, and I'm terribly proud of you."

Doc was proud too; he looked a long time at Harmony's yellow ribbon, but he was not entirely satisfied.

"Harmony's playing. He can take the jumps on the course without much trouble when he has a mind to, but he isn't trying hard enough on the high ones. Bring him out early in the morning and Chet and I will give him a workout on the high rail."

"Not with a pole, not even a bamboo one?" Pat asked anxiously.

"No, honey, but there are other ways that won't irritate or frighten him. Chet and I can hold the bar and raise it two or three inches just as you take off. That'll teach Harmony to give every rail a greater clearance than it needs. He's in only two more classes, and we've got to put our minds on it."

Pat gave Doc a bear hug that knocked off her velvet cap. He picked it up and dusted it, while she caught Harmony's bridle and led him back to the stable to cool him off.

On the next day Harmony rested. After the light workout with Doc in the morning, Mr. Lennox insisted that Pat leave him to Chet for Pat's afternoon of shopping with Mrs. Trent.

"You have your own money now, the twenty-five-dollar prize, and it would please me very much if you would spend it on a dress for the party. I talked to your mother last night after you won your prize, and she is coming Saturday to see the Jumper Stake. Jake is flying her up so she'll be here for the party. I was going to keep it a surprise for you, but I decided I'd better tell you so you can help Sarah Trent. I want you and Sarah to choose a dress for her. She's about Sarah's size. And it shall be your present to her if you want it that way. I'll just advance you the money against your next prize."

"Oh, I'm so glad for Mummy. She'll love it. She doesn't have much fun." Pat was eager to go, but she didn't know about leaving Harmony.

"Run along, Patsy. You can't work him any more today. I'll look after him, and you'll be back in time to bed him down."

It was like an afternoon in a fairy tale. Mrs. Trent let Pat linger before the displays in the marvelous plate-glass shop windows; but not too long, for there was much to do. She didn't confuse Pat with dozens of dresses, but herself selected one and asked Pat to try it on. When she looked in the mirror, Pat knew that there was no other choice. It was white, a soft floating stuff with a full skirt and a round neck and just the barest suggestion of sleeves. No puffs, no ruffles, nothing but a blue-green sash that folded over at the side with a tiny cluster of wine and yellow flowers. Mrs. Trent looked at her critically.

"Good with your nice tan. Now we must hurry to get slippers and stockings. Won't it be fun to have a whole new outfit?"

The dress they selected for Margaret was a cobweb-thin, night-blue velvet with a belling skirt and bodice and a tiny lace bolero. Pat could see her mother in it, the blue of the velvet and the black of her hair emphasizing the pallor of her heart-shaped face.

It was dark when they came out into the street and the lighted store windows gleamed with a thousand colors. Pat caught her breath. She wanted to walk down the street and stop at every window, but it was time to go back to Harmony. She knew he wouldn't settle down without her. Mrs. Trent drove her directly to the stable.

"Good night, my dear, and good luck for tomorrow."

Chapter 22

Skyscraper Stuff

The Touch and Out was scheduled for Thursday evening. In the morning Pat, Chet and Doc gave Harmony a stiff workout over a couple of five-foot jumps. In the afternoon they let him rest.

"I believe he has the idea now," Doc said. "You'll see the difference tonight."

Pat had not seen the ring under the floodlights that picked it out in glaring white and gleamed on the jewels and evening gowns of the women in the boxes. They filled her with uneasiness. Even Doc looked strange in a tuxedo. The golden girl, who seemed to understand how Pat felt, chucked her under the chin.

"Same old ring and same old people. Don't let the lights bother you."

Well, she wouldn't. She was number nineteen, plenty of time to become accustomed to them. The golden girl stayed with her for a while and told her stories about the white mare's rivalry with Lady Luck at Columbus and Detroit. Lady Luck and the white mare both had lower numbers and they both went clean; so did the bay mare that had taken fourth in the Knockdown and Out. And after Pat there were still thirteen to go. When the gate drew back for her number, her nerves were steady, and the glittering tiers of people were nothing more than a bright wall. Harmony was rested and eager, confidence flowed between them; their timing was well-nigh perfect. At only one jump did Pat fear the raucous voice of the bugle shouting a tick. The rest of the jumps were white and Harmony always had taken them easily, so she relaxed. The big chestnut, she noticed, was nervous. Once he paced himself poorly, getting in too close before the take-off, but he literally lifted himself from his hocks and finished the course without a fault.

Pat jumped down, throwing her arms around her horse.

"You're wonderful! You really got yourself out of trouble that time!"

Now for the jump-off. The course was raised to four feet six. A few minutes after the first horse entered the ring, a blast of the bugle told Pat that he had touched a jump. Lady Luck was next; she entered shaking her head to indicate that she meant business. Pat tightened her girth and was about to remount when she heard the sickening blast. Oh, no, not Lady! As he rode past her, Chet shook his head.

"It was the Oxer," he said. "Watch it."

The white mare had gone clean and it was now Pat's turn. She took a deep breath, patted her horse as she completed her circle, and headed for the first jump. With beautiful timing Harmony sailed over each jump, always looking ahead for the next challenge.

"Here comes the Oxer, boy. Steady now." Pat felt Harmony lift himself, sail over and come down to a good landing. Only one jump left—one jump! She felt a clean swish of air as they rose in a mighty arc. But was it high enough? Pat wanted to shut her eyes—every nerve was drawn tight. Harmony's front feet were over, then she felt it, the tiny shock that ran up her spine when one of his back feet ticked.

Dazed, she watched Harmony standing proudly like a statue,

posing with his red ribbon. Everybody was buzzing around her; riders who never had spoken to her before, shook her hand. Mr. Lennox and Doc were chattering as happily as a couple of magpies. She had expected Mr. Lennox to be crushed because of Lady Luck's elimination, but instead he was quite casual about it and seemed delighted to have two ribbons to his credit.

But Pat was not delighted. Harmony was no nearer belonging to her than he had been on the day Chet drove away with him. Well, maybe a little nearer; but not much. Still there was the Jumper Stake. Chet said this would be a cutthroat business for everyone was out to win, no matter how.

The next day Doc advised that they give Harmony a rest, just walking and a little trotting in the morning. Lady Luck was entered in the Scurry that night, and War Eagle in the Hunter class. Mrs. Trent asked Pat to sit with her in Mr. Lennox's box—she never had seen a horse show from the audience—but Pat didn't want to leave Harmony.

"Don't insist," Mr. Lennox said. "She has had about all she can take and needs her sleep." Pat rolled up on Chet's cot and was asleep before he and Ed took Lady Luck and War Eagle to the ring. Hours later she was dragged back to consciousness by noises in Lady Luck's stall. Doc was there and Mr. Lennox. She tumbled out to see what was the matter. One of Lady's back legs was bandaged and Doc was working on it. He looked at her and smiled reassuringly.

"She overreached and cut her pastern, but it's going to be all right. Go on back to sleep, Patsy. There's nothing you can do."

Mr. Lennox pushed her gently onto the cot. He tucked in the blanket and rolled Tip off onto the floor.

"Everything's all right, child. Shut your eyes."

Pat did. Her lids closed as though they were weighted down with millstones. When she opened them it was bright daylight and Chet was standing over her with a container of hot coffee.

"You don't need to hurry, kid. Ed's grooming Harmony."

Pat sat up and rubbed her eyes.

"Lady Luck, was she hurt last night? Did I dream it?"

"No, she got quite a cut on her pastern. She'll be all right, but it leaves the Jumper Stake up to you tonight. Mr. Lennox will be counting on you."

When Pat came back from washing her face, Doc and Mr. Lennox were in Lady Luck's stall. The mare, who paid very little attention to Doc examining her ankle, whinnied to the girl and nudged her shoulder.

"Don't feel too badly about it, my dear." Mr. Lennox smiled down at Pat. "The mare will be all right, and it's all in the day's luck. We still have a chance with Harmony. I wouldn't work him too much this morning. You don't want him to go stale."

As he left the stall he called back to her, "Your mother will be here in the late afternoon, so come home in plenty of time for dinner."

The day went in a whirl, Chet rushing back and forth between Harmony and Lady Luck, grooms and trainers swarming around the ring and the stalls, everywhere bustle and excitement. This was the big night, and Pat could feel the tension.

At the apartment there was barely time to hug Margaret. Mrs. Trent supervised Pat's dressing in the newly-cleaned and pressed habit, powdered her face and saw that her cap was at the right angle. Chet was waiting for her before they had finished the dessert.

"Keep hold of yourself. Don't rush," Mr. Lennox cautioned when he took her down to the car. "We'll be along in a little while."

He was at the ramp looking very straight and handsome in a tuxedo when Pat and Chet brought Harmony from the stall. So was Doc.

"This course is a rough one. Are you sure you know it?"

Doc asked Pat anxiously. "It's the first time you've had the Double-crossed Poles."

"I think I know it, but would you go over it with me once to be sure?"

As Pat named each jump, Doc nodded in agreement; then he thoughtfully tweaked one of her pigtails.

"Remember, Patsy, winning isn't everything—it's doing our best. Already we're terribly proud of you. So go in with your head high; and don't forget your magic word. Keep saying it to yourself and I will too. Panache, little one, panache."

The bugle sounded, the gate drew back for number one. Doc and Mr. Lennox went up to watch. The golden girl waved to Pat. This time Harmony was number seven, and Pat was glad for it was terrible to wait.

Chet moved up with her to the gate and gave Harmony's rump a pat.

"No one under four faults yet, Pat. Be careful to get him in straight for the triple In and Out. Go on, kid. You've got what it takes."

"Steady, boy, steady. It's the blue ribbon or nothing. You wouldn't want to go to the auction, would you?" Harmony seemed to understand that this was serious. He sailed over the jumps with such perfect timing that Pat felt as though she were riding on a cloud. Never except on that one bareback ride on the prairie when he had jumped the barbed-wire gate, had she and Harmony been in such perfect accord. Before she had time to realize it, they had finished the course. As the ringmaster announced, "No faults," the building rocked with cheers.

It wasn't a long wait. The golden girl went clean and came over to visit with Pat.

"We're the only two so far. It looks as though I should have poisoned you days ago." Pat smiled at her, admiring her poise. The time went quicker and her nerves steadied as she answered the girl's questions about Lady Luck. The bay and the white mare had fought for so many blue ribbons that it didn't seem right to have Lady Luck out of the ring.

"And now I have Harmony to cope with. It's always something, isn't it?" The girl laughed. "We might as well be gay about it."

"She has a magic word too," Pat thought. "I must keep on saying mine."

Finally the trumpet boomed for the jump-off. Just the two were fighting for first and second place. The golden girl was called first.

"This is going to be skyscraper stuff, but don't let it worry you." The girl put her hand reassuringly on Pat's arm. There was something so final about this jump-off. Pat suddenly began to tremble, but caught herself. This wouldn't do. She forced herself to raise her head and watch the golden girl enter the ring. A few minutes later Chet came up to give her one last word of assurance.

"That gal's doing all right. She had a hind knockdown on the last jump of the In and Out. Three faults—very good for so stiff a course." If Harmony could only do as well! But those jumps looked as high to Pat as the capitol building in Pierre.

As the gate opened for her, Chet called, "Be careful of the In and Out. It's up to four foot six, four foot nine, and five."

There was dead silence as Pat circled for the first jump. Harmony seemed to know how much this meant to both of them for he cleared the first jumps easily. As she made her turn at the far end of the ring, heading for the Double-crossed Poles, Pat began to feel confident. Harmony responded by pricking up his ears. The Hog's Back was now behind them and the four-foot-six Riviera gate loomed to the right. Up and over— Harmony cleared it, but Pat felt that he was tired. If he faltered, if he lost confidence, they would never make the dreaded In and Out. She must lift him with her own belief in him, she must give him heart; but her own courage was oozing out of her boots. She remembered the day they had brought him home and scraped the mud from his wobbling knees. She saw him struggling in the water hole, choking as the old Ford jerked and the rope blistered his neck. He had suffered too much. How could anyone expect him to win against all these sleek horses that had been fed and trained and protected since the day they were born? But Harmony was a fighter. What other colt could have lived all winter in the buttes? She wasn't going to lose him now—they had tried too hard. Nobody would love him the way she did. She just couldn't live without him.

"Panache," she muttered savagely through her teeth. She must get Harmony into exactly the right position for this last jump. As she turned him toward it, suddenly, she felt that Sketch was riding with her.

"You can do it, Patsy Pie. Of course you can." She could hear his voice somewhere inside her heart, and she knew that he was right. She and Harmony could do it. He could take this jump just as he had taken the barbed wire fence that day on the prairie. The assurance ran through her veins with a warm glow.

Harmony felt the same flow of confidence. He laid his ears forward, picked up his feet and took the first jump in stride. Pat could have crowed. She felt as light as a feather on his back. Now the second. He cleared it as easily. And the third. Why he could do it with his eyes closed. Before Pat knew it, the cheers of the crowd told her that she had won the Jumper Stake.

Pat jumped to the ground before the horse had fully stopped and threw her arms around his neck. Her eyes filled with tears and she was sobbing with happiness.

While someone was pinning the ribbon on Harmony and giving Pat the trophy, the crowd stampeded the field, photographers shouting, "Hold up your head," "Look this way," "Look that," Margaret crying, the judge from Rapid City striding through the crowd waving his ten-gallon hat, Doc smiling with the points of his moustache standing straight up. Doc hugged her so hard that he knocked out her breath.

Finally, Mr. Lennox made way for Pat through the crowd of strange faces smiling at her and kissing her, strange hands clapping her on the shoulder. Back at the apartment, Mrs. Trent helped Pat change. The girl in the cloud-white dress who stared back at Pat from the mirror looked like some creature out of a fairy tale. But there was no time to get acquainted with her. Mrs. Trent rubbed a drop of perfume behind Pat's ears and told her Margaret was waiting for her in the living room.

Margaret was sitting on the couch, starry-eyed in the blue velvet gown, and Mr. Lennox stood before the mantel smiling down at her.

"Come here, Pat, and sit beside me. I want to tell you something." Margaret hesitated as though she couldn't find the right words. "We . . . we wanted you to be the first to know. We are going to be married in the spring. We want you to be happy about it too, dear."

"Oh!" Pat caught her breath. Her head was in a whirl. She didn't look at her mother, but kept her eyes fixed on the rug to hide her confusion. She shivered and felt as though she were crumpling up inside, baffled, lost and unloved.

"You can help me train the horses, Pat. We'll be partners and raise the finest jumpers in the country. You'd like that, wouldn't you?"

Pat heard Mr. Lennox faintly. His words didn't penetrate her confusion, but his voice brought her comfort. Gradually she began to understand that she needn't worry any more. Her responsibility was over. This man would give Margaret all the solid things that Sketch never got around to. Sketch would be glad that Pat was free, that now she could do the things he had planned for her. Then one thought dominated all the others, swirling around in her head like tumbleweed in a windstorm. It steadied her and beat back the cold lonesome feeling that had clutched her throat. Harmony was hers. She had won him herself. Nothing could take him away from her now. Today was just the beginning. She and Harmony were starting out together; they might even ride in Madison Square Garden.